STARSTRUCK!

With a low hum, the lights for filming the music video clicked on. Joe, staring down from the sky-scraper at the city streets far below, took his place near an exposed ledge and waited for his cue.

"Okay, people, let's make this one count," the director shouted.

As the camera started rolling and the music began playing, Joe began to move. Then he heard a noise that was definitely not part of the video—the lighting scaffold next to him was wobbling.

"Get back!" he heard somebody shout.

Before Joe could react, a three-foot-wide light hit him squarely in the jaw and sent him flying. He grappled for balance, his arms flailing as he tumbled onto the cement sill.

His eyes fixed on the street thousands of feet below.

He was falling off the building!

Nancy Drew & Hardy Boys SuperMysteries

DOUBLE CROSSING
A CRIME FOR CHRISTMAS
SHOCK WAVES
DANGEROUS GAMES
THE LAST RESORT
THE PARIS CONNECTION
BURIED IN TIME
MYSTERY TRAIN
BEST OF ENEMIES
HIGH SURVIVAL
NEW YEAR'S EVIL
TOUR OF DANGER
SPIES AND LIES
TROPIC OF FEAR
COURTING DISASTER
HITS AND MISSES

Available from ARCHWAY Paperbacks

A NANCY DREW and HARDY BOYS
SUPER·MYSTERY ™

HITS AND MISSES

Carolyn Keene

AN ARCHWAY PAPERBACK
Published by POCKET BOOKS
New York   London   Toronto   Sydney   Tokyo   Singapore

AN ARCHWAY PAPERBACK *Original*

An Archway Paperback published by
POCKET BOOKS, a division of Simon & Schuster Inc.
1230 Avenue of the Americas, New York, NY 10020

Copyright © 1993 by Simon & Schuster Inc.
Produced by Mega-Books of New York, Inc.

ISBN: 0-671-78169-3

First Archway Paperback printing July 1993

10 9 8 7 6 5 4 3 2 1

NANCY DREW, THE HARDY BOYS, AN ARCHWAY
PAPERBACK and colophon are registered trademarks of
Simon & Schuster Inc.

NANCY DREW & HARDY BOYS SUPERMYSTERIES
is a trademark of Simon & Schuster Inc.

Cover art by Frank Morris

Printed in the U.S.A.

IL 6+

Chapter

One

WATCH OUT, BESS!" Nancy Drew shouted as her friend was almost run down by a stroller.

"Whew, that was close," said Bess, examining the tread marks on the toe of one of her sneakers.

"Sorry, miss," the mother called back as she and her toddler in the stroller disappeared into the crowd of sightseers.

"New York is one of the few places where it's so crowded you can get run over by a stroller!" Bess exclaimed as she took in the sights and sounds of Manhattan's South Street Seaport. "And I love every minute of it."

"You said it," Nancy agreed, pulling the dog-eared New York City guidebook out of the back pocket of her denim shorts. Both girls were prepared for the city's summer heat in shorts and T-shirts.

1

Behind them were the towering buildings of New York's financial district. Ahead of them were the Seaport's promenades, teeming with shoppers, tourists, vendors, and street performers. To Nancy's right was a cluster of ships, their tall white sails startling against the clear blue sky.

"Where to first?" Bess asked as a warm breeze from the East River lifted and tousled her blond hair.

"It's hard to decide," Nancy said, tucking a strand of reddish gold hair behind her ear. "It seems like every time we come here, there's more to do."

"Today might be our only day in the city," Bess said. "If I'm disqualified in the final round of judging, I'll never make it onto 'Rising Star'—and we'll be on the next plane home."

Bess had answered an ad in the River Heights newspaper asking for young performers to try out for "Rising Star," a nationally televised talent show. She was the only contestant from the Midwest picked to fly to New York for the finals.

"There's no way you'll be disqualified," Nancy said, giving her best friend an encouraging smile.

"I never dreamed I'd actually get here when I first auditioned," Bess admitted. "I'm so-o-o nervous."

"Your song-and-dance routine is so terrific, they'd have been crazy not to choose you," Nancy said. She knew Bess was more than a little worried about the final round of auditions.

They would be held the next day at "Rising

Star"'s studio at Rockefeller Center. The show had provided first-class tickets to New York and hotel accommodations for two people, so Bess had invited Nancy to go with her. Bess's cousin George Fayne had wanted to come, too, but she was busy coaching tennis at a summer camp. All she could do was promise to cheer for Bess long-distance.

Nancy and Bess had arrived in New York early that Monday morning, dumped their bags in their suite at the Astor Towers Hotel, and headed off to explore. No matter what happened with "Rising Star," Nancy knew they'd have a great time. She was especially excited because they'd arranged to spend some time with Frank and Joe Hardy, longtime friends and fellow detectives who lived in Bayport, a town outside of New York City.

"The guys are supposed to be here in an hour," Nancy said. "So we have time to check out Pier Seventeen—that three-story building full of shops."

"Shops? Shopping?" Bess's face brightened at the mention of her favorite pastime. "What are we waiting for?" She led the way across the cobblestone walk to the Victorian-style pavilion, where they browsed through boutiques filled with clothes, antique furniture, and books.

Almost one hour later, Nancy practically had to drag Bess out of a boutique so they could be on time to meet the Hardys at the waterfront.

They waited on a long wooden pier with tall

sailing ships in the background. "Take my picture," Bess said, handing her camera to Nancy.

"Say 'I'm a star,'" Nancy teased as she focused and snapped the photo. As she handed the camera back to Bess, she heard a voice from behind her say, "Isn't that Bess Marvin—the singer from 'Rising Star'?"

Nancy spun around and spotted Joe, his blue eyes full of mischief, a lock of his wavy blond hair falling onto his forehead.

"Can I have your autograph?" Joe teased.

"Forget about him—give it to me," said his brother, Frank, moving up behind Joe. At six feet one, he was just a shade taller than his younger brother.

"Frank! Joe!" Nancy exclaimed, her face lighting up as she spotted them. "Hi, guys." She hugged Joe, then Frank.

Nancy stayed in Frank's arms for just a moment longer, soaking up the sheer joy of being near him. She knew nothing could ever come of her special feelings for Frank. She had just said goodbye to her boyfriend, Ned Nickerson, back in River Heights, and Frank had a girlfriend, too. He and Callie Shaw had been going together for a long time.

"Hi, Frank," Bess said, hugging him. "And *you,*" she added, turning to Joe, "please don't talk about 'Rising Star.' My nerves are already on edge."

"I'm one of your most loyal fans!" Joe insisted,

throwing an arm around her shoulders. "Frank and I are here to give you moral support."

"We're also going to help a friend of ours out of a jam," Frank added.

"Do you mean an investigation?" Nancy asked, her blue eyes flashing at the possibility.

"Could be," Joe admitted, "but we don't have the details yet."

"I'm sorry, but we're going to have to postpone our time together until after we meet our friend Fish in Greenwich Village at twelve-thirty. That's just"—Frank paused to check his watch—"thirty minutes from now. We'd better step on it."

"But you just got here," Bess protested. "What about our Circle Line Cruise together?"

"Sorry," Joe said, playfully tugging on a curl of Bess's hair. "We'll hook up later. We've booked a room at the Midtown Hotel, since we'll be in town for a few days."

"We have a suite at the Astor Towers," Bess said. "Courtesy of 'Rising Star.'"

"The Astor Towers," Joe said. "That's star treatment for you. I wondered why you weren't staying with Nancy's aunt Eloise, but now I know."

"Actually she goes to her house in the mountains in the summer and isn't even here," Nancy added.

"How about if we meet you at your hotel—around seven?" Frank suggested.

"Sounds good," Nancy agreed. "I expect you to tell me all about your case then."

"Good deal. All Fish told us when he called last night were a few sketchy details. He's a sound engineer, and right now he's recording new cuts for a famous rock star."

"Really?" Bess's eyes flickered with interest. "Tell us who!"

Joe grinned and said, "Angelique."

"*The* Angelique?" Bess repeated. "The singer who's only our age and already has two major albums?"

Joe nodded. "You got it."

"I love her voice," Nancy said. Angelique was one of the biggest music stars in the country. Nancy had always wondered how the teenager had handled her quick shot to success. "I can't wait to hear the whole story."

Joe stepped out of the taxi and stared up at Electric Sound Studios, a windowless four-story building flanked by a small theater and a fruit stand. "You'd never guess that major stars record here."

Frank shrugged as he slammed the door of the cab. "Most recording studios don't have windows—they'd let in outside noise."

Inside, the reception area was stark and modern-looking with black leather chairs. Frank walked up to the receptionist, a woman with a wild shock of purple hair.

"I'm Frank Hardy," Frank said, "and this is my brother, Joe. We're here to see Steven Fisher."

"He's expecting you," she said. "Second floor, Studio C."

Joe followed his brother into the elevator, then glanced back at the receptionist. "Nice smile. Weird hair," he muttered under his breath.

On the second floor the Hardys passed a few open office doors. From the sound of typewriters, ringing phones, and hushed voices, Frank could hear that the offices of Electric Sound were busy.

"Check it out," Joe said, stopping in front of Studio C. The Recording light above the double doors wasn't lit up. Frank pushed through the doors.

They went straight into the recording booth with its blinking lights and knobs that resembled the control panel on a spaceship. Their friend Fish, a wiry guy with a mop of dark curly hair, was sitting in a chair behind the console. A glass wall divided the booth from the room beyond, which Frank knew was where the musicians and singers played.

"Hey, dudes!" Fish said.

"It's the Fish-man!" Joe exclaimed.

Frank noticed that Fish wasn't his usual enthusiastic self. He was biting his lip and holding the handset of a phone to his ear, while a tall, thin guy with dark brown hair paced beside him.

"Frank and Joe Hardy, meet Duke Powers.

7

Duke's the right-hand man for Crockett Skyler, the producer from Skyler, Inc., I want you to meet," Fish said.

Frank shook hands with Duke, who was in his twenties. In the room beyond the glass wall Frank saw a handful of people settling in. Dissonant sounds of guitar riffs and drum licks came from the open door to the studio. "Are you guys in the middle of a session?" Frank asked.

"I wish," Duke muttered, walking to the door and staring down the hall. "We can't seem to get this session going."

Fish rolled his eyes at the phone. "I've been on hold for five minutes, and Duke here has been wearing a rut in the floor."

"Rough day?" Joe asked, clapping his friend on the back.

Fish nodded. Back in Bayport, he'd played in lots of garage bands. When Frank heard that Fish had landed a job as an audio engineer, he wasn't surprised.

"I can't understand what's keeping him," Duke muttered. "We should be recording the basic tracks for the fourth song on Angelique's album."

"Cool." Joe was eager to meet Angelique. He had every one of her CDs.

"Is one of the musicians late?" Frank asked.

Before he could answer, Fish held up his hand and spoke into the phone. "I'm trying to track down Crockett."

Crockett Skyler, Frank thought, listening to his

friend's end of the conversation—the man Fish wanted them to meet.

"We're set to record 'Gun-shy,'" Fish said into the phone. "Seen him around?"

From the look on Fish's face, Frank knew the answer was no.

"Any luck?" Duke asked after Fish had hung up.

Fish shook his head. "No sign of him. And you tried his car phone?"

Duke nodded. "Five times. I don't get it."

"What's going on?" Joe asked.

Fish frowned as he replaced the phone in its cradle. "It's weird," he said. "Our producer has dropped off the face of the earth."

Chapter

Two

"YOUR PRODUCER IS MISSING?" Frank questioned.

Fish nodded. "The musicians are ready to go, but we can't start the session without Crockett."

"He's got to be somewhere," Joe said.

Fish shrugged. "He's not in his office at Skyler, Inc. Not at home. His secretary can't locate him. And his business partner hasn't seen him. The guy just vanished."

"Maybe he's caught in traffic," Joe suggested.

"I thought of that," Duke said, "but then why doesn't he answer his car phone?"

Good question, Frank thought. "Just how late is he?" he asked.

"The session was supposed to begin an hour ago," Fish said. "Crockett has to pay for the studio by the hour, plus wages for me and the musicians—and studio time isn't cheap."

"This is the last thing we need right now," Duke lamented. "Skyler, Inc., can't afford this— and I can't stand this waiting around." He leaned out the door, then turned back to add, "I'm going back to the office again."

Fish stared out at the musicians beyond the glass wall. "I've dealt with late musicians. Power outages. Wild tempers. But a no-show producer doesn't make sense."

"Why can't you start without him?" Joe asked.

"I'm just the engineer, hired to take care of the technical aspects of recording," Fish said. "The producer is in charge of the entire recording session. It's his money, his show. Besides, we don't have the scratch vocal tracks. Crockett was bringing them."

"Scratch vocal tracks?" Joe stared through the glass, searching for Angelique in the studio. There was no sign of the pretty, blond singer. "You mean Angelique doesn't record her part with the other musicians?"

"Welcome to the world of technology." Fish grinned. "Some albums are recorded one track at a time, which is how Angelique does it. She won't let anyone but her father in the studio while she's recording."

"Who's her father?" Joe asked.

"Didn't I tell you? Skyler's her dad," Fish answered.

"Do the other musicians use her vocal tracks as a guide?" Frank asked.

"Exactly," Fish said. "The musicians listen to

11

the scratch vocals through headsets while they record the basic tracks. It helps them to hear the melody and lyrics while they play."

Disappointed that he wasn't going to meet Angelique, Joe moved to the open doorway leading into the studio. He listened to the musicians practice. Two guys sat on stools, one tuning an electric guitar.

"That's Riff on lead guitar," Fish explained as Joe checked out the short, stocky guy with buzz-cut black hair. Beside Riff sat a tall guy with blond hair tied back in a ponytail. "Todd's on electric bass," Fish added.

In the corner was a drum set, surrounded by padded room dividers. The drummer, a thin woman with short-cropped hair and coffee-colored skin, was on her knees, adjusting a cymbal.

"A female drummer?" Joe said aloud.

Fish joined Joe in the doorway. "That's Yolanda, and Chevy's our keyboard man."

Joe glanced at the corner opposite the drum set, where a tough-looking guy with shaggy red hair and a beard played a grand piano. He wore a tank top that revealed tattoos on both of his muscular arms.

"Hey," Chevy called, "let's get started!"

"No can do," Fish answered. "Crockett's missing, and he's got the scratch vocals."

Chevy growled and banged two dissonant chords on the piano. "So why are we sitting here?"

Fish had no answer for the irate musician. Suddenly his expression changed as his eyes locked on the doorway leading to the hall.

Angelique was posed there, whipping her blond hair back over her shoulder as she glared at Fish. There was no mistaking the anger in her dark eyes.

"Where's my father?" she demanded.

"Good question," Fish said, crossing the small room and touching her elbow. "I can't reach him, and he's got the vocal tracks for 'Gun-shy.' I know you like to work alone, but the clock is running, and each minute's costing him a fortune."

Fish pointed to the studio, where the musicians were watching curiously through the glass window. "Why don't you go in there and get comfortable? I'll bring you a microphone and earphones, and just this once we'll lay down the vocals with the basic tracks."

Please say yes! Joe thought. He was actually going to get to watch one of Angelique's recording sessions!

"Are you crazy?" Angelique snapped, shrugging away from Fish. "There's no way I'm sitting through a recording session today."

Fish continued bravely, "We're in a crunch here. Can't you bend, just this once?"

A tense silence filled the room as everyone waited for Angelique's final word. Joe thought she looked even better than she did in the photos he'd seen in magazines.

"Do you really think—" Angelique began in a shrill voice, then paused and took a deep breath.

For a moment Joe thought Angelique was embarrassed as she lowered her chin and raked her fingers back through her hair.

"It won't take long," Fish said quickly. "Just a few—"

"No!" she snapped, peering through the glass at the musicians, who were watching curiously. "I can't be expected to work with those—those idiots!"

Chevy shouted, "Hey, who're you calling idiots, you—" Angelique didn't hear. She had already stormed out of the studio.

Fish rubbed his face and groaned. "Now you see why we call her the Princess," he told the Hardys.

"A *royal* pain in the neck," Frank agreed, watching Chevy gesturing angrily at Fish.

"You caught her off-guard," Joe said, defending the most gorgeous girl he had ever seen. "She wasn't prepared to perform."

Frank and Fish just shook their heads at Joe.

Just then Chevy stood up and pushed his piano bench back. "I've had it," he said in a falsetto voice. "I'm not recording with those idiots," he said, sweeping a beefy fist toward the other musicians in a bad imitation of Angelique. Laughter and applause trickled in from the studio.

Fish buried his head in his hands for a minute,

then eyed Chevy. "Don't blame me, man. I'm just the engineer."

"How about showing us how this stuff works?" Frank asked a minute later to take Fish's mind off his problems.

"Good idea," Fish agreed. He explained how everything in the studio worked, including the computer, which was used to digitally master a recording.

Fish was about to play the Hardys a rough cut of the first song on Angelique's album when the door to the hall flew open. A tall, solidly built man in his forties stamped into the booth.

"Crockett!" Obvious relief passed over Fish's face. "We were really worried about you."

Frank eyed the producer. Wearing a Western hat, T-shirt, jeans, and snakeskin boots, Crockett was dressed more like a cowboy than Frank's idea of a producer.

"He just got here," Duke said, following his boss in through the doorway.

"Where were you?" Fish asked.

"Since when do I have to account to you?" Crockett snapped. "This session is canceled—over."

"But we're all ready to go!" Fish protested. "If you just give us the scratch vocals—"

"Don't cross me. It's *canceled*," Crockett repeated, his green eyes flashing with irritation.

"Okay, okay," Fish said.

Duke backed away. "I'll tell the musicians

they're released," he said, ducking into the larger room.

Crockett dropped his tooled leather briefcase to the floor and sank into a chair. He seemed to be collecting his thoughts when he noticed the Hardys leaning against the back wall of the booth. "What are you doing in here?" he barked.

"These are the guys I told you about—Frank and Joe Hardy." Lowering his voice, Fish added, "The *detectives* I mentioned."

"I see." The hard expression faded from Crockett's tanned face. "We can't talk here. Also, I've got to get to a phone so I can attend to an emergency that's cropped up."

"How about the conference room on this floor?" Fish suggested.

"Perfect," Crockett said, picking up his briefcase and heading for the door. "Meet me there in thirty minutes. Tell Duke I'll talk to him later," Crockett said, adjusting his hat and leaving.

"I'm going to coil up the cables and put away the mikes," Fish said. He was wheeling his chair away from the console when a shout came from inside the studio.

"No way! I want my money *today!*"

Frank, Joe, and Fish rushed into the studio to try to get between Chevy and Duke. Duke's face was red, his fists clenched in anger.

"Hey, man, I told you, you'll get it later," Duke said. "Crockett gives the orders around here, so back off." He pushed Chevy back.

"You little punk," Chevy shouted as he

grabbed the neck of Duke's black T-shirt to pull him close.

"Back off," Duke repeated, taking a swing at Chevy.

"Not without my money," Chevy growled. A second later, he reached into the back pocket of his jeans and pulled out a long, narrow object.

Frank knew what it was before he heard the sickening click and saw the telltale gleam. A switchblade.

"Chevy—no," Yolanda gasped.

"Easy, man," Fish said steadily.

Chevy held the switchblade straight out, backing Duke up against the wall. "Read my lips," Chevy muttered. "Pay the money. Or pay in blood."

Chapter
Three

SILENCE FELL over the room as Chevy's fingers tightened around the knife, which he now held up to Duke's throat.

Frank noticed Duke's Adam's apple moving up and down as he swallowed nervously. "Back off, Chevy," Frank shouted, hoping the brawny guy wasn't beyond reason. "Duke can't give you your money if he's not in one piece."

Chevy responded by pressing the blade tighter against Duke's flesh.

In a second the blade would draw blood! Frank leapt toward Chevy and aimed a karate kick at the hand holding the switchblade, thrusting so that the blade would be pulled away from Duke.

Chevy groaned as Frank's foot hit his hand. The impact sent him stumbling backward, away from Duke. Even as he stumbled back he managed to hold on to the weapon.

In the split second that Chevy was off balance, Joe barreled forward and knocked him to the ground. Pinning the heavier man down with his full body weight, Joe knelt on his chest and smashed Chevy's arm against the floor.

At last the guy dropped the switchblade, and Joe clambered to his feet, picked up the blade, and backed away from the bewildered musician.

Dazed, Chevy stumbled to his feet and glared at Frank and Joe. "You'll be sorry about this," he said.

"Just get out of here before we call the cops," Duke said.

As Chevy stormed out of the room, Frank noticed that the other musicians were eyeing Duke warily.

"He's right, you know," Riff said as he closed the latches on his guitar case. The guitarist's dark eyes were grave as he faced Duke. "Crockett owes all of us some bucks. Personally, I'm going to file a grievance through the A.F.M. first."

"What's that?" Joe asked.

"The American Federation of Musicians," Riff explained. "Our union, which protects us from deadbeats."

Duke rubbed his neck and winced. "I'll see what I can do."

"Lucky for you and Crockett that tonight's gig is for charity," the bass player said as he unplugged a cord from the amplifier. "Otherwise, I wouldn't show up."

As Duke headed out of the studio, he called

19

back over his shoulder, "Save your complaints for Crockett. I'm just the middleman."

Frank decided that if Crockett was the guy they were supposed to be working for, this case would require a lot of diplomacy. Crockett seemed to be totally unreliable and behind in paying his debts.

After the musicians left, Frank asked Fish if there was any chance *he'd* be stiffed by Crockett.

"Not me," Fish said. "I work for Electric Sound Studios. The studio pays my salary even if Crockett stiffs them. Crockett has a deal with Cash Records, the company that distributes Angelique's album. They advanced him enough money for the album to pay for studio time, engineers, musicians, and songwriters."

"But Angelique writes all her own material, doesn't she?" Joe asked.

"Right," Fish said as he dropped a coil of cable into a wooden box. "So the writer's advance— and later the royalties—go to her. She may be a prima donna, but I've got to admit that her material is great."

"I'll say," Joe agreed, still sorry he hadn't been able to hear her sing.

"Is it routine for a producer to be behind in paying his debts?" Frank asked.

"Not a producer like Crockett," Fish explained. "Everyone who reads the trades, like *Billboard* and *Variety,* knows that Angelique got a hefty advance from Cash Records for this third album. That, along with the profits from her two double-platinum records, should be able to carry a few projects for Crockett."

"Then what's the problem?" Joe asked.

Glancing at the door of the studio to make sure they were alone, Fish turned back and whispered to the Hardys, "Crockett's money has run out. Someone has been embezzling the proceeds from Angelique's albums. There's hardly enough money to produce this album, let alone pay off Crockett's debts."

"Money from two albums that went double platinum?" Frank whistled through his teeth. "That's got to add up to a lot of bucks!"

Fish nodded. "And the real killer is that Angelique is turning eighteen on Friday. She'll finally have the right to control her own money —except now it's all gone."

"That's not fair," Joe said, imagining how Angelique must feel at such a lousy break.

"Uh-oh," Frank said, nudging his brother. "I've seen that look before. Something tells me that you have a special interest in this case. A personal interest in rescuing a certain princess?"

Joe grinned at the prospect. "How'd you guess?"

Twenty minutes later Fish was finished packing up the studio. "Let's head to the conference room," he told the Hardys, closing the door behind him.

In the conference room Frank and Joe sat down in black leather chairs across the table from

Crockett, who was staring at a magazine glumly. As Fish closed the door, the producer pointed to a photo at the top of a page.

"There she is," he said, sliding the magazine over to the Hardys.

"She's got two double-platinum albums," Crockett said. "Her career's skyrocketing. She's got two cuts finished on her third album—and now this mess."

"Want me to reschedule a session for 'Gun-shy'?" Fish asked as he took a seat.

"No." Crockett sighed. As he pushed back his hat, Frank noticed a ribbon of sweat trickle down the man's lined forehead. "We're going to have to put 'Gun-shy'—and the rest of the album—on hold for the time being."

"But I thought 'Gun-shy' was going to be one of Angelique's videos," Fish said. "And you need to get at least a rough mix together if you're going to deliver the video to 'Top Pop' by the end of the month." "Top Pop" was a TV show that aired hot new videos from recording artists.

"I'm changing our plans," Crockett said, holding up his hands. "We're filming the video for 'Sidewalks' tomorrow, but 'Gun-shy' is out. I don't have the scratch vocals, and Angelique can't record them now."

"No kidding," Fish muttered, then recounted what had happened when Angelique had stepped into the studio earlier. "She blew up at me," he finished.

"You were out of line," Crockett snapped. He

took a handkerchief from the pocket of his jeans to wipe his wide forehead. When he removed his hat, Frank noticed that he was bald but for a fringe of silver hair.

"I was just trying to salvage the session," Fish explained.

"You were asking her to do the impossible," Crockett said. "Angelique is suffering from larynx problems. A recording session now is out of the question."

Larynx problems. Joe began to piece things together. No wonder Angelique had freaked out when Fish asked her to sing.

"How long will it be before she can finish the album?" Fish asked.

Crockett shook his head sadly. "The doctors say that her condition may be permanent. My daughter may never be able to sing again."

Joe couldn't believe what he was hearing. Angelique was losing her voice? She was only seventeen years old!

Fish ran his fingers back through his curly hair before adding, "I'm sorry to hear that."

"It's tragic, and I think a lot of it is because of the stress over our financial situation," Crockett explained. "To make matters worse, Angelique is under more pressure because she's scheduled to sing at a huge benefit concert tonight. I've got to rig up some sort of lip-synching thing."

"Lip-synching?" Fish said, frowning. "Do you think that's a good idea? The press will destroy you if they find out about it."

"Tell me about it," Crockett said wistfully. "It would be easier to cancel, but Angelique's public appearances are so rare that this one has attracted a lot of publicity."

"Do you think the two of you can pull it off?" Frank asked.

Crockett nodded. "Duke and I can patch a vocal track into the sound system so that no one's the wiser about her problem. By the way," Crockett added, "my secretary has some extra complimentary tickets to the concert, if you guys are interested . . ."

"I'm in," Fish said. "And you guys should go for it, if you're free. It would be a good way to meet a lot of the people in Crockett's organization, Skyler, Inc."

And a great way to see Angelique again, Joe thought. "Sounds like a good idea."

Remembering their plans to meet Nancy and Bess, Frank asked for extra tickets for them. It was now time to get to the heart of the case.

"I'm not one to trust outsiders," Crockett said, swinging his briefcase onto the conference table. "But when Fish told me about you, I decided to give you boys a shot. I've got to find the thief who's robbing me blind."

"When did you first notice that money was missing?" Frank asked the older man.

"About a month ago, when last quarter's bills were to be paid," Crockett answered. "We were in the studio recording the first two songs on this album when I got the news from my accountant.

He said there wasn't enough money in my business account to cover the expenses from that session, let alone the rest of the album."

"Did you report it to the police?" Joe asked.

"Immediately," Crockett said, nodding. "They turned the case over to Treasury Department agents, who in turn put it on the FBI's docket. They haven't come up with any answers, and I can't wait for them to set aside their mounds of paperwork to work on my problem. I'm afraid the trail will be cold before the agents track it down."

How far had the government agents gotten with their investigation? Frank wondered. He decided to call his father, Fenton Hardy, an internationally known private detective who might be able to get some information for them through his friends in law enforcement. "Just how much money are we talking about here?" Frank asked Crockett.

Pushing his hat back on his head, Crockett paused before he spoke. "Two million dollars."

"Wow!" The exclamation slipped out before Joe could restrain himself. "I don't mean to sound rude, but how could so much money slip out of your account without your knowing it?"

"That, young man, is a good question," Crockett admitted. He tossed his hat onto the table and rubbed his creased forehead. "Part of the blame has to go to my accountant, Gary McGuire. He was aware that large sums of money were leaving the account by electronic transfer. But since the bank claimed that the withdrawals were authorized by me and my ex-wife, Gary didn't question them."

"You didn't notice the money missing on your bank statements?" Frank questioned.

"When do I have time to look at my business bank statements?" Crockett growled. "We're talking about Skyler, Inc.—a corporate account with hundreds of transactions a month. I trusted Gary to keep tabs on those things."

"Gary is one of the most experienced money men in the music industry," Fish explained. "No one's ever had trouble with him, and he's been keeping the accounts of recording artists and production companies for years."

"We'll need to talk to him," Frank said.

"No problem." Crockett opened his briefcase, pulled out a business card, and handed it to Frank. "McGuire has an office in the Brill Building, two floors below mine. I'll also notify my staff at Skyler and tell them to cooperate with you in any way."

As Frank took the card, a shiny silver object in the man's briefcase caught Joe's eye. He realized that he was looking at the steel barrel of a .38 revolver!

Joe was about to ask about the gun when Crockett slammed the briefcase shut.

Frank studied the card, then asked, "Before we start digging, is there anyone who you suspect could be stealing from you?"

"That's easy," Crockett said. "I can give you

someone with both motive and means. And her office happens to be right down the hall from mine—my ex-wife and ex-partner, Veronica."

"Isn't she still your business partner when it comes to managing Angelique?" Fish asked.

"Unfortunately yes." Crockett rolled his eyes. "I wish the split were complete, but according to our divorce settlement, I have to work with Veronica when it comes to Angelique's career."

"And when Veronica and Crockett are in the same room, sparks fly," Fish added.

"I taught the woman everything she knows about the business," Crockett said bitterly, "and she tried to take me for everything I've got."

"And she has access to Skyler, Inc.'s bank account?" Frank asked.

Crockett nodded. "She and I are the only ones authorized to make withdrawals. Not even Angelique can touch the money—though a lot of it is rightly hers. She was supposed to get full control of her money after her eighteenth birthday."

Glancing down at the magazine photo of Angelique, Joe asked, "Do you really think Veronica would steal from her own daughter?"

"I wouldn't be a bit surprised," Crockett scoffed. "I was married to the woman for seventeen years, so I consider myself an expert on her. Veronica is ruthless."

"I've got two shots left." Bess held up her camera, focused on a gray-and-white sea gull that had been following the boat all afternoon, and snapped a photo. "Now I'm down to one."

"Perfect timing, since we're pulling into Pier Eighty-three," Nancy said, leaning against the railing on the navigation bridge, the highest point on the boat. The boat listed slightly to port as it turned toward the large white pavilion that housed the Circle Line ships.

"It seems like we just set sail," Bess said, glancing over the docks.

"We've been on the boat for three hours, Bess. I could really go for a nice, cold drink in our air-conditioned room back at the hotel," Nancy said, grateful for the breeze that now swept along the Hudson River. The afternoon sun had been a steady reminder that it was summer in New York.

"That's for sure," Bess said, wiping beads of sweat from her forehead. "Let's see . . . I got pictures of the Statue of Liberty, South Ferry, the Brooklyn Bridge, the United Nations building, the Cloisters . . ."

"How about New Jersey?" Nancy asked, shielding her eyes and gazing at the horizon. Wispy clouds stretched over the tall buildings on the Jersey shoreline.

"Great idea." Bess pointed her camera toward the view across the river and leaned over the railing. "Wait till George sees what she missed," she murmured, fumbling for a better grip on the camera.

"What a beautiful—" Bess was interrupted as

the boat bumped against the dock. The sudden jolt knocked the camera out of her hands. "Oh, my gosh!" she gasped.

Nancy reached out to catch the camera, but it had already fallen beyond her reach.

Both girls leaned over the railing, horrified as the camera fell down to the level below.

"Look out!" Nancy shouted to the passengers below. It was too late.

With an unsettling *clunk,* the camera struck the head of a passenger. Nancy's stomach twisted as the woman crumpled facedown onto the deck, her arms spread wide.

"Nancy!" Bess cried. "I think I killed her!"

Chapter

Four

"HELP—SOMEBODY!" a heavyset woman cried out, waving her hands. "She's been hit!"

People started crowding around the unconscious woman, who wore a black tank top, denim skirt, and sandals.

"It came from up there," one man shouted, pointing up at Nancy and Bess.

"We'd better get down there!" Nancy dashed for the stairs.

"I'm right behind you!" Bess shouted.

On the lower deck they pushed their way through the crowd to where the injured passenger, a girl with dark brown hair, was sprawled on the deck. Nancy knelt down, wrapping her fingers around her wrist. "Give us some room," she ordered.

"Something fell on her from above," shrieked the heavyset woman. "It just fell out of the sky!"

"It was my camera," Bess blurted out. "I dropped it accidentally."

Nancy ignored the commotion as she felt for the girl's pulse.

"How is she?" Bess asked breathlessly.

"Her pulse is strong," Nancy told her. She leaned close to the girl's ear and murmured, "Can you hear me?" The victim didn't stir.

A crew member appeared. "Let's stand back, folks," he told the curious crowd, then turned to Nancy. "How is she?"

"Unconscious," Nancy told him. "She's probably in shock and may have a head wound. Can you get me a blanket?"

"Sure," he said, taking off and returning seconds later with the blanket. "Good thing we just docked. They've radioed for an ambulance already. The medics will board with a stretcher as soon as they reach the terminal."

"Is she all right?" one man asked as Nancy gently spread the blanket over the unconscious girl.

The crewman turned to the crowd and smiled. "It's okay, folks—let's move back and give this lady some air. You can disembark if you move toward the rear," he announced.

Many of the passengers began to turn away and file toward the aft deck.

"That's the most we can do until the paramedics arrive," Nancy told Bess, who crouched beside the girl, holding her hand.

"I feel awful," Bess said, her blue eyes shining with tears. "This is my fault."

Nancy glanced up at the few bystanders remaining. "Do any of you know this girl?"

"Not me," one man said, studying the girl's profile.

"I think she was alone," said the overweight woman in the floral-print dress. "I saw her earlier, sitting by herself near the snack bar. She seemed to be alone."

"No one was with her when she got hit," said a middle-aged man, "and I was standing right next to her."

"Did she have a purse?" Nancy asked.

The bystanders all shook their heads.

"I didn't see her carrying anything," the middle-aged man said.

As the wail of a siren grew louder, Nancy studied the victim. She seemed to be in her twenties. The petite girl was small-boned and hardly made a lump under the blanket. Her thick brown hair must have slipped out of the polka-dot band that was lying beside her.

Checking the area around her, Nancy spotted Bess's camera but didn't see any scattered possessions that might have belonged to the girl.

Just then two white-jacketed paramedics rounded the cabin. They were pulling a metal gurney and a first-aid kit. Nancy and Bess backed away so that the medical team could examine the girl.

The paramedics were taking the injured girl's

vital signs when a police officer pushed her way through the crowd, followed by the crew member Nancy had spoken to earlier.

"The police are here," Bess said, grabbing Nancy's arm. "I could be arrested," she whispered.

"Not when they find out it was an accident," Nancy said, trying to calm her friend.

The officer, an attractive woman with high cheekbones and short red hair, spoke quietly to the medics. Nancy could see her nameplate, which read Cahill. Then Officer Cahill addressed the crowd. "I'd like to speak with anyone who witnessed the incident."

"My friend and I are witnesses," Nancy said, introducing herself and Bess to the police officer. "Bess dropped her camera by accident, and it hit this girl on the head. From what I can tell, she was on the boat alone."

"I see . . ." Officer Cahill nodded as she scribbled notes on a clipboard.

"We saw *everything*," Bess said, stepping forward. "It was all my fault," she said, swallowing hard. "You see, I was leaning over the rail above, trying to get a shot of New Jersey, when . . ."

As Bess's story dragged on, Nancy turned to watch the injured girl being lifted onto the gurney. As the paramedics began to wheel her away, Nancy walked beside her. "Where are you taking her?" she asked.

"The nearest hospital, Westway," the paramedic answered.

"Can my friend and I go with you?"

"Sorry, miss," the muscular attendant said, shaking his head. "We're not allowed to let friends ride in the ambulance. Only family."

Nancy frowned as she watched the medics roll the gurney off the boat. One thing was for sure: she and Bess wouldn't rest easy until they were certain that the injured girl was all right.

Joining Bess, Nancy told her what the paramedics had said. "Let's take a cab over to the hospital."

"Good idea," Bess agreed.

"I'll give you a lift in the patrol car," Officer Cahill said, lifting her eyes from her clipboard.

Twenty minutes later Nancy and Bess were sitting on a sofa opposite Officer Cahill in the waiting room of Westway Hospital. Despite Nancy's attempts at calming her down, Bess was still upset.

"You need to relax," Officer Cahill said sternly, handing Bess a cup of water from a cooler. "From what you and the other witnesses told me, the incident was clearly an accident."

"Then why were you called to the scene?" Bess asked.

Officer Cahill removed her hat and tucked a strand of dark red hair behind one ear. "Whenever an ambulance is requested, we're called to the scene. In this case, I need to stand by until the victim's next of kin is notified."

"That is going to be difficult," came a voice

from the doorway. A doctor in a white coat stood there, his arms folded. "I'm Dr. Tong. I was called in by the attending physician because I've had experience with cases like this. The patient wasn't carrying any identification. We found these articles in her pockets," he said, handing the cop a plastic bag.

Peering over Officer Cahill's shoulder, Nancy saw that the bag contained a few loose dollars and coins, a Circle Line ticket stub, a matchbook, and a scrap of paper with writing scrawled on it. The matchbook was from Top of the Charts, a restaurant popular with musicians and record producers.

"As far as your report goes," Dr. Tong continued, "you'll have to list the patient as a Jane Doe."

"How is she, Doctor?" asked Bess.

"She's regained consciousness, though she's still disoriented," Dr. Tong answered. "Right now she's sitting up in bed, eating a snack."

"That's good to hear," Nancy said, relieved.

"Does that mean she's going to be okay?" Bess asked hopefully.

"I want to keep her overnight for observation," the doctor said. "You see, the patient has suffered a concussion, a temporary neural dysfunction that was probably caused when she hit her head on the deck. She should be fine in twenty-four hours or so."

"This *is* good news," Officer Cahill agreed. "But why can't you ID the girl, if she's awake?"

"Unfortunately, the head trauma has caused retrograde amnesia," the doctor explained.

"Amnesia?" Bess said as if she couldn't believe what she was hearing.

Dr. Tong nodded. "Our Jane Doe doesn't remember her name, address, or any of the events leading up to the accident."

Chapter

Five

"IT'S ALL MY FAULT," Bess said miserably.

"Bess, it could have happened to anyone," Nancy said, although she did feel they were responsible for the girl. "How's Jane Doe taking it?" she asked the doctor, certain that the girl must be totally freaked out, waking up in a strange hospital and on top of that having no memory of anything—neither friends nor family.

"She's pretty calm, under the circumstances," replied Dr. Tong.

"Will she get her memory back?" Officer Cahill asked.

"Usually the memory gap shrinks over time," the doctor explained. "In cases of severe trauma, the patient may suffer a permanent memory loss involving certain years of his or her life. But that shouldn't be true of this young woman. Most

37

likely her memory will return in flashes over the next few weeks."

"Mind if I have a few words with the patient?" Officer Cahill asked. "I need to interview her before I turn her case over to NYPD's Missing Persons Squad."

Missing Persons! Nancy was amazed at the twist of events that had turned an afternoon of sight-seeing into one girl's nightmare. One minute Jane Doe was a tourist, the next she was a missing person in a city of millions.

Dr. Tong hesitated, then nodded at Officer Cahill. "You can speak with her, but keep it brief. I want Jane to take it easy for the next twenty-four hours."

"Can we see her?" Nancy asked. "We're not friends or relatives or anything, but we'd like to help out in any way we can."

"Why don't you come back tomorrow?" the doctor suggested. "By then she'll be rested and better suited for visitors."

"We'll be here," Nancy promised. Already she was considering the possibility of having Jane stay with them. They'd have to extend their stay in New York. She'd talk to Bess about it on the way back to the hotel.

When Nancy told Bess her idea in the cab back to their hotel, Bess agreed immediately.

Once in their suite, they had just an hour to shower and change before meeting the Hardys at seven o'clock.

"I hope the guys are on time," Bess said as she

combed her blond hair back into a ponytail. She had changed into a pair of pleated black linen shorts and a blue tank top that brought out the blue of her eyes.

"Me, too," Nancy said. She was wearing a green oversize T-shirt, belted at the waist over a black miniskirt. She was just fastening a gold hoop earring when there was a knock at the door.

"We've had a change of plans," Frank said when Nancy answered the door. "I hope you won't be disappointed."

"Don't tell me you're backing out on us again!" Bess called from across the room.

"No. We're taking you to a concert," Joe said, fanning five bright red tickets in the air.

"You're kidding!" Bess ran over and snatched the tickets from Joe. "Tickets to Rock Charity, the big concert at Battery Park. It's been sold out for weeks."

"We have friends in high places," Joe said, grinning.

"Angelique?" Nancy asked.

"Well, not exactly. The tickets are compliments of her father, Crockett Skyler. And we've got one for Fish, who's going to meet us at the press gate."

Joe wandered around checking out the sitting room of the suite, which included antique-style sofa and chairs, a carved mantelpiece, and a view of Fifth Avenue. The suite was flanked by two bedrooms, each with its own bathroom.

"Wow," Joe said, staring at a statue on the

mantel, "pretty ritzy setup. What do they think you are, celebrities?"

" 'Rising Star' treats all its contestants like royalty," Bess said with a laugh. "But you can call me Queen Bess."

"Bess's song-and-dance number is great," Nancy said, turning to Frank. "Wait till you see it tomorrow. It's a real winner."

Bess's blue eyes sparkled as she crossed her fingers and held them in front of her face. "I wish, I wish, I wish . . ."

A block from the hotel, the teens found a diner with a jukebox and large booths. Over a dinner of fat, juicy burgers and french fries cut in long curlicues, Nancy and Bess told the Hardys about the accident on the Circle Line cruise.

"One minute she was a tourist minding her own business, the next she was out cold on the deck, not sure who she is or where she lives. All thanks to me and my camera," Bess finished, then popped a curly fry into her mouth.

"We're going back to the hospital first thing in the morning," Nancy added. "If she wants and the doctor agrees, we're going to ask her to stay with us."

"Amnesia," Joe said thoughtfully. "I thought that was something that only happened in books and Hollywood movies."

"Apparently it's very real," Nancy said.

"I can understand your concern for this—this

Jane Doe," Frank said, pushing his empty plate away. "But how can you help her?"

"I've been thinking about that," Nancy said. "If the police can't identify her, I'm going to do some investigating of my own. The least we can do is find out her name and address. Jane Doe must live somewhere."

"In a huge city like this one, an investigation like that could go on forever," Joe said as the waiter placed a check on their table.

"Not with a detective like Nancy on the case," Bess boasted. "Right, Nan?"

"I'm afraid Joe's right," Nancy admitted. "But let's hope that we get lucky. Between our sleuthing and the work of the Missing Persons Squad, we're bound to find out something."

During the cab ride downtown to Battery Park, the site of the outdoor concert, the Hardys filled in Nancy and Bess on their case. "Someone has embezzled most of the profits from Angelique's first two albums," Frank explained, recounting what he and Joe had learned from their discussions with Fish and Crockett.

"The sad part is that Angelique has seen very little of the money she's worked for," Joe explained. "Since she's singer and songwriter on the albums, she's owed most of the profits. Her parents were holding most of her share until she turned eighteen."

"Talk about long hours and low pay," Bess said, wrinkling her nose.

"Where do you think the money went?" Nancy asked.

"Great minds think alike," Frank said, smiling at his blue-eyed friend. "We're starting the paper chase first thing in the morning. Crockett's accountant, Gary McGuire, has a lot of explaining to do. I know that most businesses do their banking electronically, but millions of dollars just don't disappear without leaving some trace."

"Who's on the list of suspects—besides the accountant?" Nancy asked. She loved going over the facts of a case with Frank.

"There's Crockett's ex-wife, Veronica Skyler. Their marriage ended bitterly, and he thinks she may be out for revenge."

"Crockett may have some other enemies who might want revenge," Joe pointed out. "He seems to owe money to lots of people in the recording industry. This musician named Chevy almost knifed Crockett's assistant when he didn't get paid for today's session." He explained about Duke's close call with Chevy.

"Sounds serious," Nancy said thoughtfully. She wondered if the musicians would be willing to play for another session, knowing they might not get paid.

As the cab turned down Battery Place, Joe explained about Angelique's troubles with her voice. "She's hurt her larynx, and her doctor's not sure she'll ever sing again," Joe said.

"That's terrible!" Bess said, her eyes wide with concern.

"How's Angelique going to perform tonight?" Nancy asked.

"Her dad's going to dub in Angelique's voice," Frank explained as he leaned forward to pay the cab driver.

"And it had better work," Joe added. "Her career will be over if the press finds out she's faking tonight's performance."

In the gathering dusk Nancy could just make out Battery Park, a harborside patch of land with grassy areas and footpaths crisscrossing it. The area was alive with people and noise, and Nancy could hear the thrum of rock music in the distance.

Hundreds of people were streaming into the park. Frank, Nancy, Joe, and Bess followed the crowd to the edge of the park, where an outdoor arena had been erected. They met Fish in front of the press gate.

"This is Steve Fisher, better known as Fish," Frank said. "Meet Nancy Drew and Bess Marvin."

"Frank tells me you're in town to audition for 'Rising Star,'" Fish said as he shook hands with Bess. "You know, a lot of famous people got their first break on that show."

"I know," Bess said, smiling up at Fish. "And I'm really nervous about blowing such a great opportunity. My final audition is tomorrow."

"Well, then, this show should be a welcome distraction. Let's get in our seats before the first act comes on." They were all handed backstage passes, which were actually badges, when they turned in their tickets. "I'll give you a backstage tour after the show," he said, leading them in through the special entrance.

The steady beat of taped music pounded out over the excited chatter of the audience. Soon after an usher led the gang to their seats in the third row, the lights dimmed.

A hush fell over the arena, and a moment later the stage lights came up and the emcee bounded on stage.

The show featured six rock celebrities who had volunteered to perform for free. Joe thought all the acts were good, but couldn't wait to see Angelique take the stage.

"When does Angelique come on?" Bess asked as Mario Slick, a rock guitarist, took a final bow.

"She's up next," Fish answered.

As soon as the emcee announced Angelique, the audience went crazy. Electricity charged the arena. Screaming fans stood on their seats and waved their arms. Other people pushed their way up the center aisle. Frank saw two of the plain-clothes security guards at the foot of the stage tense, on alert. The crowd spilled forward right up to the lip of the stage, then seemed content to remain there.

Onstage, Angelique appeared in a circle of light. Her blond hair hung wild and loose around her shoulders, and her red lips curved in a mischievous smile.

When the music started, she swayed slowly to

the beat and the audience roared. Light glimmered over her skintight copper-colored bodysuit as she strutted across the stage.

"She's dynamite," Joe told his brother.

Frank nodded, staring at the stage. He recognized two of the musicians from the recording session earlier that afternoon. Riff danced into the spotlight for a guitar solo, while Todd thumbed the bass in the shadows.

Fish tapped Frank on the arm and pointed at the stage. "Looks like Crockett's plan is working."

Crockett's plan? It took Frank a second to remember that Angelique wasn't really singing. With the lights, music, and noise from the audience, it was hard to tell.

"Tell your friends it's me you love. . . ." Angelique cooed as the music rose.

"Tell your friends it's—"

Suddenly the sound was cut. The lights went out. Only the murmur of confused voices filled the darkness.

"What's going on?" Bess cried.

"The power's out," said Fish.

A moment later a shrill scream cut through the night, then was lost amid the sound of a mob advancing.

"They're storming the stage!" Frank shouted as the crowd erupted in pandemonium.

Chapter

Six

A NGELIQUE!" Joe jumped onto his chair, trying to make out what was happening on stage. In the darkness the only thing he could see was the mob swarming down the center aisle.

"The crowd is out of control!" Nancy cried.

Joe jumped down from his chair. "I'm going up to help her," he said, heading for the center aisle.

"Whoa," Frank said, grabbing his brother by the arm. "This way." He yanked Joe toward the side aisle, which wasn't so packed.

His eyes adjusting to the available light from the moon and street lamps, Joe scrambled to penetrate the densely packed mob, but Joe hadn't spent afternoons on a football field without learning a few aggressive plays.

Adrenaline pumped through his veins as he

elbowed his way past a stocky kid with spiked hair. Finally he reached the edge of the stage.

With one arm, he vaulted onto it and spun toward center stage, where Angelique was cowering—only to come face-to-face with one of the burly security guards.

"Get down," the guard growled, his fist drawn back.

"Yeeow—wait! I'm on your side," Joe shouted, pointing to the backstage pass that was stuck to his shirt.

A few emergency work lights came on just then, and the beefy guard squinted at the pass as Joe explained that he worked for Crockett. "All right. Go on," the man muttered, joining ranks with other guards and stagehands to hold off the crowd at the foot of the stage and restore some order.

Joe finally got to center stage, where a small knot of fans had made it to Angelique.

Todd, the bass player, was there tugging on one guy's arm, trying to get him to leave the stage, while Riff was arguing with another overzealous fan.

Then he saw Angelique—caught between two other guys. A stocky kid with a red kerchief over his head had thrown his arm around her, and from the look on Angelique's face, he was too close for comfort.

"Excuse me," Joe said, trying to sound official, "but Crockett Skyler has asked that the band meet him backstage."

Riff and Todd spun around and acknowledged Joe. "Gotcha," Todd said.

The guy with the red kerchief wasn't budging. "Angelique wants to stay with us, don't you, Angie?" He gave her a tug that threw her off balance.

She hesitated. "I think I'd better—"

"She's staying with us," said red kerchief.

Thinking fast, Joe glanced into the wings and pointed to a stagehand. "Is that—I can't believe it, but it's got to be him. I wonder what Spyder Monroe is doing here?"

That caught their interest. "The Spyder?" Red kerchief glanced over, loosening his grip on Angelique. "Where?"

"There—" Joe pointed to a short, thin guy with brown hair and round tinted glasses. He did look like the famous rock star Spyder Monroe. "The guy with the leather vest on."

As the two fans turned toward the stagehand, Joe gently took Angelique's hand and led her to the opposite wing.

"You don't know me," he whispered in her ear, "but I was at the studio when you stopped by today. I work for your father. I'm Joe Hardy."

"Thank goodness." She reached out and grasped his arm for support. "For a moment there, I was afraid you were another wild fan. Now I remember why I don't do concerts."

From close up Joe could see the strain on her pretty features. There was a hollow look to her round brown eyes, and her red lips were pressed together into a tight line. Still, she was gorgeous —and at the moment she was clutching his arm!

"Angelique!" Crockett rushed up to them then. "I was afraid you'd be eaten alive out there."

Despite the producer's words, Joe thought Crockett seemed more flustered than concerned.

"Almost," she said, smiling at Joe. "But Joe saved me. Thanks. I owe you one." Then she rose on her toes and planted a kiss on his cheek.

Yee-owza! Joe's face heated up at the touch of her lips. As he watched her duck into her dressing room, he realized that he must have a smear of red lipstick on his face. At the moment he didn't care one bit.

Just then the stage lights went on, and Joe could hear the audience applaud and cheer.

"Hey, Hardy!" Fish called. As Joe looked up, his friend emerged from a passageway that led to the backstage exit. "They've found the source of the problem. One of the electricians told me that some jerk disconnected the main line to the generator out back."

"Looks like they've fixed that," Joe said, "but what about Angelique?" He didn't want to say it aloud, but he was wondering if anyone would remember that Angelique's vocal track had to be rewound and cued up.

"No problem," Fish said. "I ran into Crockett, and he's taking care of it."

A few minutes later Angelique was composed and ready to face the audience again.

"Tell your friends you're my guy . . ."

Angelique swayed in time to the music. Even after the disruption, Joe thought she gave a dazzling performance. He felt lucky to be watching from the wings.

"She's great, isn't she?" he said, nudging Fish.

Fish studied Joe's face, then broke into a smile. "Aw, man—you got it bad."

"You just can't resist playing the hero, can you?" Frank told Joe as they went in the front door of a rock club called the Assembly Line.

"Hey—" Joe gave his brother a wounded look. "I managed to get us an invitation to the stars' party, didn't I?"

"I'm impressed," Nancy said, taking in the cavernous room illuminated by constantly moving searchlights. "This place is enormous."

"It used to be a factory," Fish explained. "See those conveyor belts? They use them to send stuff in and out of the kitchen now." He led them to an iron spiral staircase. "Come on up. The second-floor loft is reserved for our party."

Upstairs the party was in full swing. Nancy squeezed past a group of girls with beehive hairdos and heavily painted faces and followed Fish to an empty table at the left.

Bess pulled out a chair and sat next to Nancy. "Get down," she said, nodding along with the steady hum of rock music that filled the air.

Joe and Frank elbowed their way through the crowd and took the empty seats beside Bess.

"Angelique's not here yet," Fish observed, eyeing the crowded room.

"Wait till George hears that we partied with Mario Slick and Angelique," Bess said. "And it's all because of you, Joe."

Joe grinned, remembering how Angelique had kissed him. "Although that blackout turned the concert into a pretty strange event," he said.

"Why would anyone want to turn off the power?" Nancy asked.

"Maybe it was some kid, pulling a prank," Bess suggested.

Fish shrugged. "Well, it would have to be a smart kid—and one familiar with how a concert is set up. The wiring gets technical. You don't just turn off a single switch."

"It was obviously someone who knew his way around backstage," Frank said thoughtfully.

Before anyone else could comment, Bess changed the subject. "Look," she said.

Nancy followed her glance over to the buffet table, where two hunky guys in tight jeans were loading up their plates. One of the guys had the letters *R-I-F-F* carved into the back of his black hair.

"Aren't those the guitarists from Angelique's band?" Nancy asked.

"Todd and Riff," Fish said, nodding. "If you want, I'll introduce you."

"Look over there," Bess cried, throwing a hand over her heart as she stared at a handsome black-haired man on the dance floor. "It's Mario Slick! What a heartthrob."

"Be still, my heart," Frank muttered sarcastically.

"Down, boy." Nancy laughed, punching him in the arm. Although she wasn't as impressed as Bess, she could see why women liked Mario. Even offstage he seemed to radiate energy. He was dancing with a petite woman with angular features and straight reddish brown hair.

Just as the song ended, Fish waved at the dance floor. "Hey, Mario, over here," he shouted.

Mario looked over at Fish, then took the hand of his dance partner and cut through the crowd to join him.

"How's it going, Fish?" Mario said, smiling at everyone at the table.

"Great," Fish said. "I want you to meet my friends Joe and Frank Hardy, and their friends Bess Marvin and Nancy Drew."

"This is a total thrill," Bess said, standing up to shake Mario's hand.

"Hey, the thrill's all mine," Mario said, flashing her a smile. "And this is my manager, Veronica Skyler."

Angelique's mother? She looked younger than Frank had expected, and up close she resembled an older version of Angelique, with darker hair.

"How're the plans for your autumn tour going?" asked Fish.

"We've just about ironed out all the details,"

Veronica said, "so we decided to celebrate to-night."

"Sounds good," Frank said.

Veronica was already turned away and waving to someone across the room. "It's that reporter from *Rolling Stone* who called today," she said, nudging Mario. "She'll do a blurb about the tour."

Mario nodded, then grinned at the gang. "We'll catch you later."

Frank watched as the couple disappeared in the crowd. "I wonder what Crockett thinks about his ex-wife working so closely with Mario Slick?"

"I know what you mean," Nancy said. "From the romantic looks that passed between those two, I have a feeling there's more to their relationship than business."

Just then the crowd surged toward the main door. "She's here," one girl shouted, rushing off the dance floor to join the crowd.

"The princess has arrived," Fish said dryly as the others watched Angelique enter the room. Frank saw that she was acting very friendly, taking time to chat with fans, reporters, and photographers. Was she really as spoiled as Fish made her out to be? Duke Powers and Crockett flanked her on either side, acting as her body-guards.

"Did you like the show?" Angelique called to a fan. "First time I ever blew the lights out."

"She sounds fine," Frank told his brother. "I'm surprised that she can talk at all."

"Yeah," Joe said. Crockett had made it sound as if Angelique's larynx condition was serious. Maybe it only affected her singing, he thought. One thing was sure—she looked terrific. She was shaking hands with a fan when her brown eyes locked on Joe.

"Here's my hero!" she exclaimed, rushing over and squeezing Joe's arm. He introduced the pretty singer to Frank, Nancy, and Bess, then explained why Bess was in town.

"'Rising Star'!" Angelique shrieked. "Lucky you. Maybe you'll be discovered, Bess."

Bess shrugged modestly. "I'm just hoping to make the final cuts," she said.

"Your friend here could be another rising star," Angelique said, squeezing Joe's shoulder. "Joe's going to be in my new video."

"I—I am?" Joe felt his throat tighten as everyone stared at him.

"You are. It'll be great," Angelique said. "After you saved my skin at the concert, I couldn't get you out of my mind. Then, when we were in the limo driving over here, it hit me. I said to myself, 'You *must* get that guy in your video.'"

"But I'm not a dancer," Joe said. "And I don't sing or—"

"Don't worry, Joe. You just need to be your hunky self," Angelique insisted.

"But I really don't—"

"You'll be great." Angelique clapped him on the back. "We're shooting tomorrow afternoon at the Chrysler Building. We won't need you till around four. Be there?"

Joe nodded, unable to think of any way to say no to Angelique.

Frank watched as the singer continued across the room. "A star is born," he said to his brother.

"Are you going to do it?" Nancy asked.

"Of course I am," Joe replied. "How could I let Angelique down?" He grinned.

Fish shook his head and smiled. "I see that the princess has cast her spell on you."

Angelique settled in with her entourage at a small table in the corner of the room. She did indeed remind Frank of a princess holding court.

"What's up?" Fish called as Todd and Yolanda passed by. Fish introduced the blond bass player and the pretty drummer to everyone at the table.

"We were just about to hit the dance floor," Todd said. "Anybody want to join us?"

"Sure," Bess said, pushing her chair back.

"Sounds good," Fish said, joining them.

As she watched them head over to the dance floor, Nancy heard angry voices behind her. She turned and saw Mario standing at Angelique's table, yelling at Crockett. Veronica was off to the side, glaring at her ex-husband, while Angelique just sat quietly, staring at the tabletop.

She nudged Frank. "Looks like he's getting carried away," she said, watching as Mario jabbed a finger at Crockett. The party seemed to stop as everyone stared at the men.

"Back off," Crockett shouted. "You'd still be waiting tables if it weren't for me!"

"That's it." Mario's hand closed around a soda bottle on the table. "Old man, you just went too far."

A moment later the sound of broken glass exploded through the air as Mario spun around and smashed the bottle against the brick wall. With deadly resolve, he gripped the neck, its jagged edges toward Crockett.

His black eyes glistening with rage, Mario slowly stepped toward the older man. The broken bottle neck glimmered as he growled, "You'll pay me my money—the money *you* owe me. Or I'll be carving my name on your face."

Chapter

Seven

"WAIT!" NANCY SHOUTED at the men as she jumped to her feet.

Frank was right beside her. "Mario," he said calmly, gazing into the singer's crazed eyes, "put the bottle down."

"Not till I get my money," Mario said, jabbing the broken bottle at Crockett.

"Come on, folks," Joe said, tensed to spring if Mario took action. "I'm sure we can settle this without a fight."

"Hey, cool it," Crockett growled. "You'll get your money, but not here. This is a party." He glared at Mario, then looked at Veronica, who was smiling at him. *"She* put you up to this!" he exclaimed.

Although Mario didn't respond, Veronica's smug smile told Nancy that Crockett was probably right. She must really hate him, she thought.

"No mind of your own?" Crockett egged the rock star on.

Frank saw Mario tense beside him, preparing to lunge at Crockett. "Mario, let it go for now," Frank murmured. "You need to have Crockett in one piece—so he can pay you."

At last Mario lowered his arm and tossed the jagged bottle neck to the floor. "Don't think you're off the hook, Skyler," he spat. "Until you turn over the money you owe me, I'm going to be your worst nightmare." His black eyes glittered as he scowled at the producer, then turned and walked out the door.

Angelique jumped up from the table and ran toward an Exit sign at the far end of the loft.

"I'm going after her," Joe told his brother. "Maybe I can help pick up the pieces and see what's really going on." When Frank nodded, Joe cut across the dance floor and followed Angelique outside. Frank turned back to Crockett, who didn't seem to notice that his daughter had left.

"I've had enough," the producer said, pushing back his seat and picking up his leather briefcase. "I'll speak with you tomorrow," he told Frank, then headed out the door.

Some father, thought Frank, watching the waiter sweep up the broken glass by the wall. Frank's eyes skimmed the room, where the dancing and laughter had picked up again. Veronica was sitting at an empty table across the room, staring down into her drink.

She, too, seemed more concerned with herself than with her daughter. "This is probably as good a time as any to talk with the other half of Skyler, Inc.," Frank told Nancy. Together, they wove a path through the crowd on the dance floor.

"Mind if we join you?" Frank asked, pulling out a chair at Veronica's table.

When the dark-haired woman nodded, he and Nancy sat down.

"I know you're friends of Fish," Veronica said, eyeing Frank and Nancy critically. "Are you on Crockett's payroll?"

"Not exactly." Lowering his voice, Frank explained that he and Joe had been asked to investigate the embezzled money.

"Well, good luck," Veronica said bitterly. "Don't get me wrong. No one wants to see that money recovered more than I do. But you're on a wild-goose chase. If I know Crockett, he's buried that money somewhere. He's squirreled it away for himself."

"But the missing money is causing Crockett problems," Nancy said, recalling Mario's threat. "Why would he pretend to be broke?"

"That's easy. He wants to keep the money out of my hands," Veronica said through clenched teeth. "He's convinced himself that he launched Angelique's career all by himself. He could never have done it without me. But he refuses to share the credit—or the profits."

"But what about Angelique?" Frank asked.

"Would Crockett cheat his own daughter out of money she earned?"

A sad expression came over Veronica's delicate features. "I used to think that Crockett had Angelique's best interests at heart. At one time she was the apple of his eye," she admitted wistfully. "But that's changed. The only thing Crockett cares about is himself. He'd sacrifice our daughter for money."

Frank wondered suddenly if he was working for the wrong person.

Meanwhile, Joe had followed Angelique out to a terrace on the flat roof of the old factory. The "princess" was in the midst of a royal tantrum. Fortunately, beyond a few potted plants, which she had kicked over, there weren't any breakable items on the terrace.

Joe hung back, watching as Angelique kicked and pounded on the wooden railing. Then she folded her arms on the balcony rail and burst into tears.

Joe stepped through the doorway. "Hey, it can't be that bad," he said softly.

Angelique lifted her head dolefully. Her eyes were red and puffy from crying. "Yes, it can," she said.

Not sure what to say, Joe patted her gently on the back. "This stuff will blow over," he said, thinking of the argument between Mario and Crockett. "When my brother and I track down the missing money, all these problems will be solved."

"No they won't," Angelique said, wiping a tear from one cheek.

"Yes they will," Joe said. "Your father has asked us to help. My brother, Frank, and I are detectives."

"Really?" Angelique's eyes opened wide. "That sounds exciting."

"It's okay." Joe grinned, glad that Angelique seemed to be feeling better. "But not as exciting as being a rock star."

Angelique frowned, and Joe realized he'd said the wrong thing.

"Stardom isn't as glamorous as people think," she said. "While other kids are going to parties and proms, I'm holed up in a recording studio. Sometimes I think I'd give it all up just for a chance to spend a day on the beach or go on a camping trip with my friends."

Joe had never considered how much a teenager would have to give up for fame. He felt bad for Angelique. "Sorry to hear about your throat problems," he said. "Does it hurt to talk?"

"No." Angelique touched her neck gently. "But I can't sing."

"But your larynx will recover with rest and you can pick up where you left off," Joe said.

"If I had my choice, I'd run away from this career—and never look back!" Angelique exclaimed. From the determined expression on her face, Joe could see that she meant it. Could her life really be that bad?

"But what about your music? Wouldn't you miss composing and singing?" Joe asked.

"Not much," Angelique murmured. "I'd give it all up for the chance to break the ties with my parents. If I had the money from those double-platinum albums, I'd take the next flight to some secluded island, drop out of sight, and leave my parents to work out their problems without dragging me into the middle!"

It didn't sound like such a bad idea, Joe thought. "Sounds like their divorce has made things kind of tough for you," he said.

"Ever since they split up, it's been horrible. They're my managers. They're my parents. But whenever they disagree on something, I get stuck between them."

She stared down at the street below, watching cars cruise along the West Side Highway. "I'd love to know which one swiped my money."

"Wait a minute," Joe said. "Do you really think that one of your parents is the embezzler?"

Angelique nodded. "Talk to our accountant, Gary. He'll tell you the same thing. My parents are fighting a war, and I'm just the major casualty. They don't care that I've worked for years without the right to spend much of the money I earned. Now that I'm turning eighteen, it's all gone."

Joe felt sorry for Angelique. The picture she painted of her family and career was bleak. She also had the additional burden of figuring out which of her parents was cheating her out of millions of dollars!

"Hey, Hardy!" Joe turned around to see Fish standing in the doorway. "We're ready to head out. You coming?" Fish asked.

"In a minute," Joe called.

"I'd better go, too," Angelique said, reaching out and squeezing his hand. "Thanks for listening. I'm sorry if I dumped all my worries on you."

"Anytime. And I'll see you tomorrow at the video shoot," Joe said, following Angelique inside. He knew people thought she was a spoiled brat, but with all the pressures on her, it was a miracle that she managed at all. Some life, he thought.

Downstairs, Joe, Frank, Nancy, and Bess said their goodbyes and piled into a cab for the ride back to their hotels. Just as the cab started to drive off, Angelique's bass player, Todd, ran outside and shouted, "Now, don't forget what I told you about keeping cool on stage, Bess."

"I won't," Bess shouted, waving goodbye. "I can't believe it's almost one A.M.," she said. "I hardly had a chance to circulate at the party."

"I don't suppose a blond bass player named Todd had anything to do with that," Nancy teased.

"All he did was give me tips about my audition on 'Rising Star,'" Bess protested. "And I also got an earful about how recording sessions work.

Can you believe Todd has *never* been in the studio with Angelique?"

Frank nodded. "With today's technology, a lot of groups record their tracks separately."

Bess sighed. "What happened to the magic?"

"From what Angelique told me, the magic has been lost for a long time," Joe said. He told the others what he had learned from the young singer. "She's so upset about what her parents are doing that she's ready to walk away from her career."

"It must be horrible for her, wondering which of her parents is cheating her out of the money she's earned," Nancy said thoughtfully. She had noticed that neither Crockett nor Veronica had appeared concerned about how the arguing was affecting their daughter.

Thinking over what Joe had said, Frank was struck by an idea. "From the way she kept talking about running away with the money, do you think that might be her plan? Do you think *she's* the one siphoning off the money?"

"Is it possible?" Nancy asked. "I thought she didn't have access to the money."

"We'll check it out tomorrow morning, when we go over the books with Gary McGuire," Joe said, though he doubted that pretty, golden-haired Angelique was capable of embezzlement.

"It'll be busy tomorrow, with Bess's audition at noon and Joe's video session at four," Nancy said.

"Fish told me they're using a helicopter for the video," Bess said. "They're going to film Angelique on the top of the Chrysler Building."

Frank smiled. "Imagine, my little brother's face plastered on TVs across the country." Then he and Nancy filled in Bess and Joe on Veronica Skyler. "She claims that Crockett is the one stealing the money," Frank finished.

"That's no surprise," Joe said. "Throw in Mario, the mad guitarist, and this case resembles a full-scale rock 'n' roll war."

The next morning Nancy and Bess ate breakfast in the Astor's coffee shop, then headed off to Westway Hospital to meet the girl known as Jane Doe.

"Good morning," Bess said brightly as she and Nancy paused outside the open door of the semiprivate hospital room.

"Hello." The dark-haired girl was sitting up in bed, a glass of orange juice in her hand. Her shoulder-length hair hung loose, and the color had returned to her face. Nancy was glad to see that at least she looked healthy.

"Do I know them?" The girl turned to Dr. Tong, who was standing beside her bed. Another man with bushy brown hair was also there, jotting down notes on a clipboard.

"These are the young ladies I told you about," Dr. Tong explained. "Bess Marvin and Nancy Drew."

"We came back to see how you're doing," Bess said. "Feeling better?"

"Much better," the girl answered, smiling.

"In fact, she's going to be released this morning," said the doctor. "As soon as Detective Lebowitz is finished." He nodded at the man with bushy hair and a beard. "He works for the Missing Persons Squad."

The detective glanced up at the girls. "Just finishing up some paperwork on Jane," he said. At the mention of the name *Jane,* Nancy noticed the patient's eyes light up, as if she remembered something.

She said, "Jane—that name. How do you know my name?"

"Sorry, miss," he said gently. "But the police department will refer to you as Jane Doe until we find out your real identity."

"Oh, I see," Jane said, obviously perplexed.

Maybe Jane *was* her real name, Nancy thought.

"That about wraps up the paperwork, except for a photo," Detective Lebowitz said, lifting an instant camera. "Here we go." He paused as a flash lit the room and he snapped the girl's picture.

While waiting for the photo to develop, the detective explained, "We'll distribute this picture throughout the police department, then release it to the press. Once it hits the newspapers and TV news shows, there's a better chance that someone will come forward and identify you."

Jane's mouth dropped open as he spoke. "The

press!" she gasped, turning pale with fear. "But you can't do that."

"It's standard procedure—" the detective began to explain.

"No, please don't," Jane pleaded desperately. "If you print that picture, I'm—I'm as good as dead!"

Chapter

Eight

E ASY, JANE, EASY," Dr. Tong said. "No one's going to force you to do anything." Then he turned to the detective and added firmly, "I can't have you upsetting my patient."

"Sorry, miss." Detective Lebowitz put the camera down on the nightstand and scratched his head. "But this is one of the fastest ways we know of finding out who you are."

"You can't do it," she insisted.

"Try to remember," Nancy said gently, taking Jane's hand, "why you're afraid to have your photo publicized. Is there someone who might want to hurt you?"

Everyone watched as Jane rubbed her eyes, trying to concentrate. "I'm not sure—" She hesitated. "I remember a man—and a gun. I was running. I was scared. The man was dangerous. I think he was trying to kill me."

"Can you describe this man?" asked Detective Lebowitz.

Jane closed her eyes tight, then opened them. A tear ran down her cheek. "No, I can't picture a face. All I can remember is the gun." She turned to Dr. Tong. "Am I going crazy? Could I be remembering a nightmare?" Her voice was full of fear.

"If the memory is this vivid, it's probably real," the doctor reassured her. "Clinically speaking, amnesia victims are sometimes paranoid. But even if you just think you're in danger, I wouldn't recommend releasing the photo."

"We don't have to run it," Detective Lebowitz said, "though if we don't, my job is going to be more difficult."

"If the photo jeopardizes Jane's life, it's not worth releasing it," Nancy said firmly.

Jane's recollection of danger seemed to fit in with something that had puzzled Nancy all along. "You were found without a purse or wallet," Nancy said. "Maybe you were mugged. Maybe someone snatched your bag at gunpoint?"

"Does that ring a bell?" Lebowitz asked.

"I just don't know," Jane said. "I don't know anything," she whispered sadly.

"But you will—we'll help you," Nancy said.

Detective Lebowitz tucked his pen into his clipboard, then handed Jane the photo he'd taken. "Let me know if you change your mind about releasing this photo. Your case will stay open, but I can't make any promises. I've already checked the files on people reported as missing, but you don't resemble any of the profiles."

At this Jane looked as if she might break down.

"Jane," Nancy said, "Bess and I would like you to stay with us."

Bess jumped in, explaining about the huge suite provided by "Rising Star." "There's plenty of room, and Nancy can help you piece things together as your memory comes back. She's a detective, with a pretty good record for solving cases."

"Is that right?" Lebowitz said dryly. He fished a card out of his pocket and handed it to Nancy. "In that case, we should stay in touch. I'll expect to hear from you, especially if Jane starts to piece together her identity."

"Of course," Nancy agreed, and she gave Detective Lebowitz their hotel room number.

Dr. Tong turned to Jane. "I'm glad you're going with Nancy. If she hadn't suggested your going with her, you'd have to go to a shelter. Now, I don't want you to worry if you're depressed or feel emotionally numb for a little while. Your memory should start coming back, though—in brief flashes at first. Just be patient."

"Is there anything I should do?" Jane asked.

"Get plenty of rest, and check in with me in a few days. If you need to talk to me earlier, just call the hospital and they'll page me," Dr. Tong said, patting Jane's hand. "The nurse will be in with release papers for you to sign. And then you're free to go."

"That's good," Bess said, checking her watch. "Because I have an important date at Rockefeller Center. I've got to be onstage in an hour."

As planned, the Hardys walked over to the Brill Building that morning to investigate the financial angle of the missing money.

When the secretary showed them into the office of Gary McGuire, Joe did a double-take when he saw the short, thin man with glasses shaking his brother's hand. The guy seemed familiar.

"It's a pleasure— *You!*" Gary shoved his glasses up on his nose and scowled at Joe. "You're the guy who put those groupies on my trail last night at the concert!"

In a flash Joe remembered. "Sorry about that," he said. "I was trying to save Angelique."

Frank was confused. "What's this about?"

Joe explained about the fans who'd been muscling Angelique. "The only way I could shake the creeps loose was to send them after our friend here, Spyder Monroe."

"Nice trick, brother," Frank said.

"Not for me," Gary snapped. "Those jerks practically mauled me. Thanks a lot."

"Sorry," Joe said, shrugging.

"I hope you're not as irresponsible in your work," McGuire said, taking a seat behind his desk.

What about you? Joe wanted to ask, but his brother's warning look said, "Back off."

"Crockett asked me to give you a copy of Skyler, Inc.'s transactions for the past year. The printout's almost complete," said the accountant.

Joe followed the man's gaze to a computer in the corner of the office. The printer was spewing out sheets of ledger paper onto a fat stack. "It's as thick as a brick!"

"Don't worry," McGuire said. "I'll have my secretary messenger it over to your hotel so you won't have to lug it around."

Joe wasn't bothered by the prospect of lugging around a sheaf of paper; he hated the prospect of sifting through it!

Unlike his brother, Frank was eager to dig in and study the details of Skyler, Inc.'s setup. Maybe they'd find a clue or pattern indicating how the money was being embezzled. "While the printer's finishing up, maybe you can answer some questions," he suggested.

"Sure." Gary gestured to the two chairs in front of his desk. "Have a seat."

Just as the brothers sat down, there was a knock at the door. Before Gary could answer, Crockett poked his head in. "I see you guys have met. These boys need our full cooperation, McGuire."

"Whatever you say," Gary said, opening a folder. "While you're here, I have some paperwork that needs your signature."

Crockett crossed the room and signed his name on three papers. "Any news?" he asked.

"We're just getting into the nuts and bolts of the investigation," Frank explained.

"Don't let me interrupt. I'll catch up with you later," Crockett said, ducking out the door.

Frank decided to lead in with a general question. "Do you handle all the finances for Skyler, Inc.?"

"Yes," Gary said. "I keep tabs on the earnings and costs of each artist's recordings. I write the checks for Skyler, Inc., which represents a number of artists—including Angelique and Mario Slick."

"I guess you've heard that Mario's determined to get his money," Frank said.

McGuire shrugged. "Skyler, Inc., owes Mario ten, maybe twelve thousand dollars. The corporation could cover a check to Mario, but Crockett's put a hold on all payments."

"So he's not really broke?" Joe asked.

"No. There's about forty thousand in the account. But how do you divide that up when you've got Mario making threats, and Angelique and Veronica demanding their shares? Not to mention the fees for studios and musicians on Angelique's new album. Now it seems that album isn't going to be completed."

From what Frank had seen at the studio the day before, he had to agree. The news didn't seem to bother McGuire, though.

"And the feds have no leads?" Joe asked.

Gary snorted. "The feds are kind of restricted by laws in other countries."

"I know you've gone over this for federal investigators," Frank said, "but I'm confused. Can you explain how the money disappeared from Skyler, Inc.'s account?"

"It started with one withdrawal slip." Gary went to a metal file cabinet, opened a drawer, and pulled out a manila folder. "This single withdrawal was never authorized, but it showed up on the bank statement. I'm sorry to say I didn't catch it right away, but the way Crockett spends money, I didn't really notice until I actually did the books a month or so ago. By that time the account didn't even have enough money to cover expenses. That was when I started backtracking. I called the bank and was able to get a copy of this withdrawal slip." He handed it to Frank.

Joe leaned over Frank's shoulder, and his mouth opened wide in surprise. "But it's for only a thousand dollars!"

"And it's signed by both Veronica and Crockett," Frank said, studying the slip. "Were the signatures forged?"

Gary shook his head. "Have a look at this contract. The signatures are exactly the same."

Frank and Joe checked both sets of signatures and had to agree.

"The bank says they're authentic, too," Gary said.

"Even Crockett and Veronica agree, though they don't recall signing the withdrawal slip. If it's a forgery, it was done by a master." The accountant sighed.

"So that was the first withdrawal," Frank said, handing the slip back to McGuire. "Where are the others?"

"You'll find them listed in the printout, but there are no more withdrawal slips." Gary adjusted his glasses nervously, then added, "After the first withdrawal, the money was removed by electronic transfers. Today a lot of banking is done electronically—by computer or phone or fax machine. Someone ordered that two million dollars be transferred from Skyler, Inc.'s main account to another account, which had been set up with this thousand dollars as the initial deposit."

Noticing that the printer had stopped, Gary picked up the sheaf of paper and dropped it onto his desk. "Here, I'll show you." He leafed through the printout and pointed out several transfers of varying amounts totaling two million dollars.

"That's crazy," Joe objected. "How can someone withdraw millions of dollars without a signature?"

"Once a bank has a signature on file," Gary said, holding up the withdrawal slip, "they will authorize the withdrawal of money without question. The signatures also eliminated the possibility of its being someone on the staff at the bank."

"So why can't you just get the money out of the new account and replace it in the old one?" Joe asked.

"The catch is," Gary explained, "when we

checked to see where the electronic transfers went, the printout from the bank was marked Confidential. After that it listed this code word—PIKA."

"That doesn't tell you anything," Joe said, frustrated.

"No kidding," Gary said sarcastically. "That's why we're having such a problem. The bank officers said that the thousand dollars was transferred to a confidential trust account *outside* the U.S. The rest of the money was electronically transferred to that same account. But all we have to go on is this cryptic code—PIKA. The federal agents are trying to track it down, but with strict confidentiality laws in other countries, it's very difficult for them to find out anything."

"But we're talking about millions of dollars," Joe pointed out.

Frank nodded, adding, "How could so much money disappear without anyone's noticing?"

"Crockett's always been a big spender. It's his style to withdraw money without accounting for it properly. Classic cars, in-ground pools, antiques . . . About a year ago I questioned several large withdrawals he made—see, he withdrew money without telling me what it was going for—and the man went crazy. But this time, when I had to pay quarterly bills, I noticed the account was about to be overdrawn."

"Why didn't you warn him sooner?" Joe prodded.

"I'm an accountant, not a financial therapist. I

tried to counsel Crockett a year ago, as I told you, and he almost fired me. So this time I followed his instructions."

"You could have said something to Veronica," Joe said. "Isn't she an equal partner?"

McGuire rolled his eyes. "Crockett is the money man in Skyler, Inc. I deal with him exclusively. Also, they don't pay me enough to brave the war zone between those two." Gary glanced at his watch and stood up. "I've got an appointment with a client across town. Can we wrap this up?"

"We don't want to keep you," Frank said politely. "But we'd like to stick around and look through the Skyler, Inc., files if we could."

"You're not going to find anything that the feds didn't," Gary said.

"One last question before you go," said Frank. "Who has access to Skyler, Inc.'s accounts— besides Crockett and Veronica?"

"No one," Gary said. "Those two are the only people with banking privileges."

After Gary left, Frank skimmed his printout, while Joe set to work perusing the files marked Skyler, Inc.

"What do you make of McGuire?" Joe asked.

"You mean, besides the fact that he hates you for siccing fans on him by calling him Spyder Monroe?" Frank said. "I wouldn't want him handling *my* money."

"What am I looking for?" Joe asked. He wasn't crazy about the digging part of any investigation.

"Just keep an open mind," Frank answered,

concentrating as he studied the columns of numbers on the printout. "We need to cover all bases. Maybe we'll find a pattern in the withdrawals."

As far as Joe was concerned, the files of tax returns, bank statements, and ledgers revealed nothing. "I'm wasting time," he complained. "Why don't I check back with Crockett? Or better yet, I'll talk to Veronica. Didn't Crockett mention that her office is just down the hall from his?"

"Yes," Frank said. "All the Skyler, Inc., officers are on the twelfth floor. When I spoke with Veronica last night, she just pointed the finger right back at Crockett."

"Maybe you just didn't ask her the right questions," Joe said, closing the file drawer.

Frank stared at his brother. "And you think *you* can charm some information out of her?"

Joe grinned. "Her daughter seems to like me."

Sighing, Frank gave in. "Go on. It's the only way I'll ever get anything done around here."

Upstairs, Joe found Veronica's office door ajar. When he knocked, the door opened all the way, revealing a room filled with plants and antique furniture—but no Veronica.

Glancing down the hall, Joe made sure no one was watching before he ducked into the office and closed the door behind him.

He crossed the room and sat down behind the huge mahogany desk. Although he found nothing unusual in the bottom drawer, he smiled to himself. It was a lot more exciting to search places where he hadn't been invited.

In the top drawer he found a travel folder. Inside were tickets to the Cayman Islands—one for Veronica and one for "M. Slick." Mario Slick! Was Veronica secretly working with Mario against Crockett? It had seemed that way the night before.

Joe didn't have time to think his theory through. The sound of a woman's voice outside the door gave him a jolt of adrenaline. Veronica!

"I'll just be a minute—" she called.

As the doorknob turned, Joe sat behind the desk, feeling like a duck caught in the sight of a rifle.

He was trapped!

Chapter

Nine

THERE WAS NO TIME to think. In one fluid motion Joe shoved the tickets into the drawer, closed it, and dropped to his knees. Veronica was already pushing open the door when he crawled into the kneehole of the desk.

His heart was hammering hard in his chest. Would she notice that a few things were out of place? Joe could only squeeze into the dark shadows under the desk and wait.

"Let's see," she murmured.

Peering out from his hiding place, Joe could see only Veronica's high-heeled shoes and shapely legs as she opened and closed the door of a credenza behind the desk. There was a pause, during which the desk chair moved, and Joe held his breath, fearing that the woman was about to sit down. Fortunately, she didn't.

A minute or two later she walked back to the door, and it sounded as if she'd gone out. Joe didn't hear the door click shut, so he waited for a minute to avoid coming face-to-face with Veronica. Finally sure it was safe, he crawled out, stood up, and stretched.

That was close, he thought as he glanced over the items on her desk. He'd take a quick look through her appointment book and files, then make a beeline back to McGuire's office.

"Bess is so nervous about the audition," Nancy confided to Jane as they munched on sandwiches. "But she'll be fine if she just relaxes a little."

Inside the "Rising Star" studio at Rockefeller Center, the final auditions were about to begin. Bess was backstage with the other contestants. On the set, friends and crew members milled around a buffet table. With plates in hand, Nancy and Jane had found seats in the section of the studio where the audience sat during each taping.

"I'm sure she'll be great," Jane said. "I want you to know that I think it's really nice of you and Bess to give me a place to stay. I don't know what I'd do if I had to stay in the hospital or go to a shelter. Right now I'm kind of numb, as if this is all a bad dream."

Nodding sympathetically, Nancy said, "We'll stay with you until you piece things together. Don't try to force anything." She couldn't imagine how upset her father would be if she should suddenly disappear.

"I've been thinking about my family," Jane said. "And somehow I'm sure I don't have any relatives in New York. I could be wrong, but I remember a sister in Minnesota. At least, I think she lives there." Jane shook her head, frustrated. "How am I ever going to piece my life together?"

"We can start by going over the things in your pockets," Nancy suggested. "I know you don't have any identification, but there was a note with some writing on it. Do you still have it?"

Jane reached into the pockets of her denim skirt. She found the scrap of paper Nancy had mentioned and unfolded it. A few lines were scrawled on the crinkled page.

Shoot the moon.
Shoot the sky.
Leave me out.
I'm gun-shy.

"It looks like a poem," Nancy said.

Nodding, Jane studied the writing thoughtfully. "Maybe I'm a poet—or a writer."

"Gun-shy," Nancy said, reading the last line. "I wonder if that has anything to do with your memory of a gun."

"I'm not sure, but I don't think so." Then all at once an expression of terror crossed her face. "I do remember a loud bang. Gunshots . . . and bullets." She shivered. "He was chasing me, hunting me down—"

"Calm down," Nancy said. "He's not here now. You're safe. Nothing's going to happen."

As the tension slowly left Jane's face, Nancy wondered who could possibly have wanted her dead—and why? Could the poem have anything to do with it?

Nancy was still thinking about it when she heard a drumroll. Brandon Winkler, the host of "Rising Star," dashed onstage and greeted the audience. He had a mustache, blond hair, and perfect teeth. Viewers across America loved him.

"For our first audition," he said, smiling at the small audience, "let's welcome a dynamite lady from the Midwest, Miss Bess Marvin!"

Nancy held her breath as the curtain opened, revealing one of her best friends. Bess's black-and-white-striped oversize shirt and black tights resembled the uniform of a football referee. "Bess, stay cool," Nancy whispered, feeling almost as nervous as if she were onstage.

Then Bess started to sing, her voice strong and clear. Nancy relaxed. Bess was doing better than she'd ever done before!

"He'll run a play right down the line, then break your heart before halftime," Bess sang about a romance with a football star.

The stage lights made the sequins on Bess's shoes sparkle as she kicked into the air, stepped back, and pivoted in a whirling spin.

"She's doing great," Jane whispered.

Nancy hoped the judges felt the same way.

Frank stared at the computer screen in Gary McGuire's office. He'd finished searching through the printout and files without learning anything new. Feeling as if he'd hit a dead end, Frank noticed that the computer had been left on.

What luck, Frank thought. He had access to Skyler, Inc.'s files without having to boot up or key in a password. Of course, no one had invited him to go through the computer files, but Crockett had promised him full access.

Frank sat down at the terminal and keyed in a request for a list of the files. A list of more than a dozen files filled the screen. He pulled up the files one by one, scanning for anything that seemed unusual or out of place.

In a file called SLICK, he found a detailed accounting of Mario Slick's first album. The numbers confirmed that Crockett owed the man a little more than twelve thousand dollars.

Other files contained information on expenditures. Frank whistled as he scrolled through the data. Crockett had spent thirty thousand dollars of Skyler, Inc., money on a gun collection. And his swimming pool had cost more than a hundred thousand dollars. The expenditures weren't illegal, but they were extravagant. Bet Crockett would give anything to have that hundred thousand in his pocket now, Frank thought.

Just then Joe returned and closed the door behind him. "That was close." He dropped into a chair, recounting how he'd had to hide from Veronica. "I did find some surprises. Including a pair of plane tickets. She's going to the Cayman Islands on Saturday with—guess who?—Mario Slick."

Frank whistled through his teeth. "Very interesting. What else?"

"I went through her appointment book," Joe said, taking a folded piece of paper out of the pocket of his jeans. "I jotted down some of her appointments, thinking that we might want to keep an eye on her. She's got a dinner date tonight at Top of the Charts. Lunch tomorrow at Grazi's."

The computer beeped, and Frank glanced at the screen and read: ACCESS DENIED. PASSWORD?

He tried to pull up the file again but got the same response. "That's strange," he told his brother. "There's a lock on one of the files."

Joe joined his brother at the terminal. "It must contain confidential information."

Frank tried to access the file again, but got the same annoying beep. Finally he gave up.

Then he turned to his brother. "Did you say that Veronica and Mario are going to the Cayman Islands?" he asked thoughtfully.

Joe nodded.

"The Cayman Islands are an international banking center, where no one asks you any questions when you open an account. It's almost impossible to get any information regarding a person's private account there, too," Frank said.

Joe nodded and said, "Some people hide their money there because the islands have so few banking regulations and no taxes."

The two brothers stared at each other. "Are you thinking what I'm thinking?" asked Frank. "That there's a connection between that trip and the missing money? Like, maybe they're going to collect some of the dough from an account named PIKA?"

"I think it's time we talked with someone who may be more familiar with this case," Frank said. "Federal agents have been working on it. Let's make some calls to see if one of Dad's friends can help us out."

Half an hour later Frank was in touch with one of the agents working on Crockett's case. Although Special Agent Paul Thornberg refused to discuss the case on the phone, he listened to what Frank had to say about his suspicions that the money was in an account in the Cayman Islands.

"A friend of mine has done some investigative work on Grand Cayman," Thornberg told Frank. "Let me give him a call to see what he can turn up." Before he hung up, Thornberg agreed to meet with the Hardys the following day.

"Two o'clock tomorrow, in his office," Frank told his brother.

Joe nodded. "Ready to go? We'll have to hurry to catch Bess's audition for 'Rising Star.'"

"We can head out just as soon as we put these files away," Frank said. "But let's check in with Crockett before we leave."

Quickly Frank and Joe straightened up McGuire's office and went out to the elevator.

Two floors up, Crockett's office door was closed, and his secretary was away from her desk. Frank knocked on the door and waited. No one answered. "Maybe he's gone to lunch," he said, rapping on the door a second time.

Easing the door open, Frank peered inside to see papers fluttering through the air. His eyes locked on the figure of a man standing behind Crockett's desk, where files were spread open. The man was fumbling with papers, frantically shoving them back into a folder.

Expecting to see Crockett, Frank was surprised to find himself staring into the angry black eyes of Mario Slick.

Chapter

Ten

"Mario! What are you doing here?" Frank asked, stepping into the office.

Frank already had his answer, though—Mario was combing through Crockett's files. Startled by the knocking, he'd tried to replace the papers, but hadn't had enough time.

"Is Crockett with you?" Mario asked, tilting his head so that he could see behind Frank.

"No." Frank stepped aside so that Joe could enter. "It's just us."

"Good. Let's keep it that way," Mario said as he closed a folder. "I'm here to get the numbers. Crockett says he owes me twelve thousand dollars, but I think it's a whole lot more. Somehow he's been fixing the books. I'm going to find out how and nail him."

Recalling how violent Mario had become the

night before, Frank didn't want to push the guy.
"And have you found what you're looking for?"

Mario nodded. "I've found my statements,
and believe me, *my* accountant will go over them.
If there's one thing wrong, I'll sue Crockett for
every penny he's got." He extracted a page from
one file, folded it, and tucked it into his jacket
pocket. "The guy is dirty. His accountant's dirty.
But I'll get my money if I have to squeeze it out of
him one penny at a time."

Was it possible that Gary and/or Crockett had
been dummying the books? Frank wondered.

"Hey," Joe said, "we'll try to get to the bottom
of this. But in the meantime, I suggest you stay
out of other people's offices."

"I'll leave him alone once he deals with me
fairly," growled Mario. "I somehow doubt that
will happen, though. See, I know about the
missing money—and you don't need to look too
far to see who took it."

"Really," Frank said.

"Skyler did!" Mario exclaimed. "I have an
inside contact!"

"Veronica Skyler?" Frank prodded.

Mario smiled. "Very good. I hope you're just as
good at finding what Skyler did with the missing
money. That way I'll have a better chance of
getting what Crockett owes me." He gathered up
the scattered files, shoved them into the drawer,
and slammed it shut. "Later."

Joe watched Mario disappear out the door. "I

guess I wasn't the only one snooping around the Skyler, Inc., offices today."

When Crockett's secretary returned from downstairs, Frank and Joe discovered that the producer had already left for the video shoot.

"I guess we'll see him later," Joe said. He was taking a step forward when the door to the reception area opened and Fish strode in.

"Hey, dudes," Fish said, stopping at the secretary's desk. "Just got an emergency call from Crockett. He needs a copy of 'Sidewalks' over at the shoot. I've got to find the rough mix and get a copy over to him."

The secretary rolled her eyes. "I don't know where it is. Look on the shelf beside the tape deck." She pointed toward Crockett's office.

The Hardys followed Fish into the office, where dozens of cassettes were stacked beside a tape deck. Fish ran his finger down a row of plastic cassette cases, then groaned. "What a drag. Crockett's not too organized." He chose a tape and popped it into the player.

The sweet, low voice that poured out was unmistakably Angelique's, though Joe didn't recognize the song. "Is that the mix you're looking for?" he asked Fish.

Adjusting the volume, Fish shook his head. "No, but this is the first cut from the new album. It's called 'My Broken Heart.' Angelique wrote it. What do you think?"

Joe nodded in time to the music. "Catchy."

The second song was called "Words," but it

still wasn't what Fish was looking for. At last, he found the rough mix of "Sidewalks." "Gotcha!" he said, ejecting the tape. He tucked the cassette into his shirt pocket. "Gotta run. Crockett needs this right away."

"We'll see you at the video shoot in a few hours," Joe said.

Fish smiled. "See you there, hotshot."

As the Hardys walked over to Rockefeller Center, they discussed the details of their case.

"I think we can assume that the embezzler got Crockett and Veronica's signatures on the first withdrawal slip so that they couldn't charge that the bank made a mistake," Frank said. "Unless the Skylers are working together to steal the money, which I might have suspected if I hadn't seen them together. It's clear that they can't stand each other."

"Then there's Mario," Joe added. "He and Veronica are close, and now that Veronica's representing Mario, they're a team. From the way he talks, they'd love to leave Crockett in the dust while they rake in the bucks on Mario's autumn tour. I say we keep an eye on them."

"Good idea." Looking down the block, Frank could see the sign for Radio City Music Hall on Avenue of the Americas. "In the meantime, we shouldn't limit our suspects."

"Though we know that Crockett and Veronica are the only people with access to the Skyler, Inc., account," Joe pointed out.

"True," Frank agreed. "But you said it yourself

—security at Skyler, Inc., is lax. You made it into Veronica's office, and Mario walked right into Crockett's. The place is wide open. A lot of people could have found a way to get their hands on company records—such as withdrawal slips. Including Angelique."

Joe thought about the singer. He didn't want to believe she was a thief, but he had to keep an open mind. Even if the girl was a knockout.

"Ladies and gentlemen, I'm pleased to announce a most unusual event." Brandon Winkler paused as he glanced at the contestants who were lined up beside him onstage.

In the audience Nancy and Jane sat with their fingers crossed for good luck. Nancy was sure that Bess had dazzled the judges, but the other contestants had performed well, too.

"In the category of female vocalist, we have a tie between Luisa Lopez and . . ." Brandon glanced at the card in his hand before adding, "Bess Marvin!"

Bess and the other contestant stepped forward and bowed as the small audience applauded.

"Now, because of the format of our show, we can feature only one female vocalist on Saturday's broadcast," Brandon Winkler explained. "So we'll give our contestants an hour to prepare themselves for a tie-breaking performance."

A tiebreaker? Nancy wasn't familiar with the rules. She hoped Bess had prepared two songs.

The host thanked the rest of the performers,

then the audience gathered at the foot of the stage to congratulate and console the contestants. Bess frantically motioned Nancy and Jane to a door off to the side of the stage.

The girls met in the wings and quickly found an empty rehearsal room to use for the next hour. One wall of the room was covered with mirrors. The rest of the room was sparsely furnished with folding chairs and an upright piano.

"I can't believe it!" Bess moaned as she sat down behind the piano. "What in the world am I going to sing?"

"Oh, Bess," Nancy said, sighing. "Didn't you rehearse another song?"

Jane sat down beside Bess and played a few chords on the piano. It was clear that she was familiar with the keyboard.

"Wow." Bess smiled, despite her problem. "You know how to play the piano."

"And you're fairly accomplished," Nancy said, leaning against the piano. "What's that song you're playing?"

Jane didn't answer. Instead she sang, her voice deep and clear and full of emotion. Something had clicked—Nancy was sure of it. Jane was spellbound, totally absorbed in the music.

When Jane struck the final chord, Bess applauded.

"Music must be an important part of your life," Nancy said quietly.

When Jane raised her head, Nancy saw tears glimmering in the girl's dark eyes. "That song is close to my heart. I even remember how down I was feeling when I wrote it." She sighed, then ran her fingers over the keys.

"It's a beautiful song," Bess said glumly. "I wish *you* could perform the tiebreaker for me."

Jane spoke simply. "You know, Bess, the lyrics of that song are easy. I'll bet you could learn them in twenty minutes."

Bess's blue eyes lit up as she took in what Jane was telling her. "Do you think so? Oh, I'd love to sing it!"

"Sure," Jane promised. "And I'll back you up on the piano."

"This'll be great," Bess said, moving up to the piano. "Now, how does the song begin?"

An hour later the tiebreaker began. Nancy sat in the studio bleachers, watching as Luisa Lopez sang a country song.

When Luisa was finished, Nancy looked down at the judges in the first row to see their reaction. One woman was wiping a tear from her eye. What if the judges chose Luisa over Bess? Nancy pushed the thought from her mind. No way, she told herself.

Then it was Bess's turn. She and Jane came on stage. Biting her lip, Nancy watched. "Come on, Bess, you can do it," she whispered.

"My broken heart," Bess sang soulfully as Jane played, the piano music a soft accompaniment. Suddenly Nancy's concentration was interrupted by the sound of footsteps behind her. She turned and saw the Hardys moving up the aisle toward her. She waved to them, then quickly turned back to Bess.

"They're in the middle of a tiebreaker," she whispered as they sat down beside her. "I'm so nervous I can't stand it!"

"She's doing great," Frank said, already caught up in the performance.

Joe was wrapped up in the song, too, but not because of Bess's abilities. There was something about the lyrics that didn't seem right.

"You'll find another love, make a new start," Bess sang. "And leave me alone with my broken heart."

"'My Broken Heart'?" Joe whispered. That was the song that Fish had played for Frank and him. "Where did Bess get this song?" he asked Nancy.

"Jane taught it to her," Nancy whispered, nodding at the dark-haired girl playing the piano.

"That's impossible!" Joe insisted, trying to keep his voice down. "This is the song we just heard on Angelique's tape," he told his brother.

Frank listened closely, then nodded. "You're right, but the song hasn't been published or released yet. So how did Jane get her hands on Angelique's material?"

Chapter

Eleven

SHH!" NANCY WHISPERED, adding, "We'll talk about it after Bess's audition is over." She was positive Joe had made a mistake and didn't want to miss a second of Bess's performance.

As Bess was singing, Joe listened carefully. Note for note, word for word, he was sure it was Angelique's song.

"Yeah!" Frank whooped as Bess took a bow and Nancy led the audience in a standing ovation.

The second Bess and Jane left the stage, Nancy said, "Come on, let's go backstage."

They found Bess pacing the floor of the rehearsal room, while Jane played a soothing melody on the piano. Back in the audience, Nancy knew, the judges were tallying their scores.

"How'd I do?" Bess asked.

"You were great!" Nancy said, hugging her friend. Then she turned to Jane and said, "And so were you."

"Thanks for coming, guys," Bess said to Frank and Joe, then introduced Jane to the Hardys.

"I seem to be running into a lot of detectives lately," Jane said, shaking her head.

"That was a beautiful song you played out there," Frank said. "Do you know who wrote it?"

"I did," Jane said proudly.

When the brothers exchanged a doubtful look, Nancy intervened. "That song may be our first clue to your identity, Jane," she said gently. "Frank and Joe heard the same song on a tape by the rock star Angelique. It's called 'My Broken Heart,' and Angelique claims that she wrote it."

Jane frowned, her brown eyes confused. "Angelique? The name sounds familiar, but I *know* I wrote that song." After a pause she added in a strange voice, "My memory is hazy, but for some reason my connection to music is strong. And 'My Broken Heart' belongs to me."

The intensity of Jane's reaction convinced Nancy that the girl was involved in music in some way. "I don't know what the connection is," she said, studying Jane, "but maybe someone in Crockett's organization could help us out." She told Jane that the Hardys were working on a case for Crockett Skyler, the producer of Angelique's albums and the girl's father.

"You know, Jane, you have a fabulous voice,"

Bess said. "Maybe you were a backup singer for Angelique? That would explain why you know 'My Broken Heart.'"

"I don't think that's it," Jane said, perplexed.

"I've got an idea," Joe said. "The video shoot for Angelique's new album is going on right now. We were heading over at four, but we can go early. Why don't you come with us?"

"I can't go anywhere until the winner is announced," Bess said, pacing. "How long could it take to tally a score?"

"Bess, it's only been a few minutes," Nancy said, although she was almost as anxious as Bess.

Frank turned to Jane. "Can we count you in for the video shoot? There's a chance that someone there will recognize you."

Jane shook her head and huddled on the piano bench, hugging her knees to her chest as if for protection. "I don't know. I'm kind of tired. And I'm not sure I'm ready to meet people." She turned to Nancy and asked, "Do you think it's safe?"

Nancy frowned. She couldn't blame Jane for being wary—especially if images of guns and bullets and hunters danced through her mind. "Maybe you should take it easy," Nancy suggested.

"Why don't you come back to the hotel with me?" Bess told Jane. "Nancy can go with the guys and ask around."

"Better yet," Nancy said, recalling the photo

Detective Lebowitz had taken, "I can show people your picture and see if anyone recognizes you. I won't offer any details that would help the wrong person locate you."

Jane found the photograph in the pocket of her skirt and handed it to Nancy. "I'm willing to try it," she said. "If I don't take a risk, I'll never fill in the gaps of my memory."

Just then Brandon Winkler appeared in the doorway, a bright smile on his face. "Bess Marvin? Get ready to appear on 'Rising Star'!"

"I won the tiebreaker?" Bess squealed, clapping her hands in disbelief. When Brandon nodded, she jumped in the air. "All right!"

"Report here on Thursday for camera blocking," Brandon said. "The director will want to run through your routine and choose the best shots for the cameras. Pick up a schedule before you leave."

"I'll be here," Bess promised.

"Congratulations," Nancy said, hugging Bess.

Bess was still beaming when the group left the studio. Bess and Jane headed back to the Astor Towers, while Nancy and the Hardys hailed a cab to the Chrysler Building, which was on Lexington Avenue.

On the way over, Nancy told the Hardys about Jane's memory of a man chasing and shooting at her.

"Now I understand why she seemed scared," Joe said.

Nancy nodded. "She wants to discover her identity. But at the same time, she's afraid it will lead her into the path of a killer."

"A tough situation," Frank agreed. "But if she remembers things like guns and bullets, I'd say it's serious. Better to play it safe than to risk Jane's life."

The cab pulled up outside a building embellished with art deco molding. "This is it," Frank said, handing the driver a few bills.

Joe climbed out of the cab and staggered back to stare up at the towering facade. "We're filming at the *top* of this? I forgot how tall it is. No wonder they need a helicopter."

"The Chrysler Building was the world's tallest when it was built, in 1929." Nancy was reading from her guidebook. "It was designed to celebrate the Golden Age of Automobiles. The spire at the top is shaped like the front grille of a car. And see those gargoyles?"

Frank shielded the sun from his eyes as he moved back and tried to look up. "I can't see them from here, but I remember they're shaped like hubcaps. Pretty cool."

Inside the lobby, Frank told the security guard that they were with Crockett's staff. The guard called upstairs to get clearance, then showed Nancy and the Hardys to a special elevator that would take them to the old observation lounge. "Watch your step when you get up there," the guard warned them. "It's cluttered with equipment and cables."

"Will do," Frank said, nodding at the guard.

"I hope Angelique isn't afraid of heights," Joe said as the elevator doors closed.

"Maybe she'll want to cry on your shoulder again," Frank teased his brother over the hum of the elevator.

Joe didn't answer. He wasn't sure if the queasy feeling in his gut was from the elevator ride or the idea of seeing Angelique again.

When the elevator stopped, the doors slid open to reveal what looked like a wild party. The floor was littered with TV transmitters and electronic gadgets. Joe saw dozens of people uncoiling fat cables, speaking into walkie-talkies, and rolling a camera into position. The teens got off the elevator and stepped over cables beside two racks of clothes.

"What are we going with next?" a wardrobe assistant shouted over a rack. "Leather or lace?"

Rounding a large, dish-shaped transmitter, Frank spotted Fish and Duke standing next to a scaffold of giant lights.

"How's it going?" Frank asked.

"We're taking a break while Angelique changes and touches up her makeup," Duke said.

"Duke's working as a production assistant," Fish explained, clapping him on the back. "He's in charge of communications between the crew here and the cameraman on the helicopter."

"And what's your job?" Nancy asked Fish.

He shrugged. "I'm off the payroll for the

moment. I had to drop off a cassette earlier and decided to hang around and watch."

Scanning the cluttered space, Joe spotted Angelique sitting in front of a lit mirror wedged against two black curtains strung on a temporary scaffold. She leaned back and closed her eyes as a stern-faced young woman with spiked blond hair dabbed a small sponge over her pale face.

"Where's Crockett?" asked Frank.

"You just missed him," Fish said. "He had to go downtown to board the helicopter at the landing pad."

"We spent the last hour shooting close-ups," Duke explained. "In the next segment we'll add a second camera, shooting from outside the building. Crockett wanted to check out the shots through the remote camera. Once we're ready to shoot, we'll radio the copter and do a few more takes."

"Too bad Crockett's not here," Nancy said, reaching into her tote bag. "We thought he might help us identify the girl in this photo." She showed Fish and Duke the picture of Jane.

"She doesn't look familiar," Fish said, shaking his head.

Duke studied the photo, then shrugged. "Never met her. What's her story?"

Joe said, "The weirdest thing happened. It's got to do with Angelique's song and this girl. She's—"

"She's a real fan of Angelique's," Nancy finished for Joe, catching his eye so he wouldn't tell the story. Then, choosing her words carefully, she explained that Jane was suffering from amnesia. "We're trying to help her piece her memory back together," she finished.

"Tough break," Duke said, then his walkie-talkie began to crackle. "Excuse me." He turned away to answer the portable radio.

At about the same time Frank noticed Gary McGuire sitting at a table, leafing through some papers. "That guy's the accountant for Skyler, Inc.," Frank whispered to Nancy.

She nodded. "Let's try him." Frank and Nancy showed the accountant the photograph.

"How do you know this young lady?" Gary asked, his brow wrinkled in concern.

Briefly Nancy told him how she and Bess had met Jane. "Do you know her?"

"She looks familiar, but I can't say from where." He paused, then added, "It's good of you to help out such an unfortunate girl."

He seemed so troubled that Nancy decided to probe a little more. "Maybe she had an interview with Crockett that you overheard," she suggested. "Would you—"

"Mr. McGuire," interrupted an assistant, who handed Gary a stack of bills.

"These invoices should have been submitted last week," McGuire said, leaving the table to chase after the assistant.

Meanwhile Joe had wandered over to talk with Angelique, who was smiling as the makeup artist brushed on a coat of pink blush.

Frank and Nancy joined them and Frank interrupted when there was a pause in their laughter. "We could really use your help with something," he told Angelique. "Nancy's trying to help out a girl she met yesterday."

When Angelique heard the story of the girl's amnesia, she said, "How awful. Let me see her picture. Give me a little space," she directed the makeup artist.

Nancy handed her the photo, and Angelique's smile faded. "Her!" she exclaimed, tossing the photo onto the makeup table. "What is this? Some kind of joke?"

"Then you know her?" Frank said hopefully.

"I wish I'd never met her." Angelique scowled. "That girl is a no-talent groupie. She used to hang around my father, trying to get work. He tried to help her, even gave her a shot in the studio, but she couldn't cut it. Pressure was too much for her. She ruined every take and cost my father a lot of money."

"She used to work for your father?" Nancy asked.

Angelique nodded. "And she was bitter when Dad fired her. That girl is nothing but trouble."

"Are you sure?" Nancy said, shocked by Angelique's description. Having heard Jane sing that afternoon, Nancy knew she was talented, and she found it hard to believe that mild-mannered Jane could have caused so much trouble.

Could amnesia alter a person's character and

talent? Nancy would have to check with Dr. Tong.

Frank asked Angelique what the girl's name was.

The blond star wrinkled her nose. "I—I don't remember. You try to forget a nightmare like her."

"Well, if the name comes to you, give me a call," Nancy said. "I'm staying in Suite Seventeen-twelve at the Astor Towers."

Duke appeared, his walkie-talkie crackling. "Excuse me," he said, "but you should be changing and getting into makeup."

"That's right." Angelique smiled at Joe. "We'll be using the extras in the next segment."

The wardrobe mistress gave Joe a pair of holey black jeans, a black leather vest, and black combat boots to put on. "Do I get to keep the outfit?" Joe joked, admiring himself in the mirror.

Next it was time for makeup. "Have a seat," Duke ordered, pushing Joe into a nearby chair. "After Zoe paints you up, we'll need you to sign a contract and release form."

The makeup artist began sponging flesh-colored liquid all over Joe's face and neck—then applied a pencil to accent his eyes and a brush with peach powder blush to his cheeks.

Frank stared at his brother in the mirror. "It's amazing what a coat of paint can do." Joe threw him a punch, which Frank dodged.

Duke returned with a clipboard. "Read these over and sign on the bottom," he said, handing

Joe the clipboard. Joe read the contract and release and signed his name.

"Okay, people," someone shouted. "Let's get going. We're on the clock."

"That's our director, Judd Sachs," Duke said, pointing out a short man with curly brown hair and a full beard. "Where do you want the extras?" he asked.

Duke led Joe and the other two extras over to where Sachs stood behind a lighting scaffold. Joe gazed up at the wide ladder of metal rods that held a dozen lights. The lights pointed toward an arched floor-to-ceiling window opening that led directly outside and was cordoned off temporarily with tape.

Joe walked over to the arched opening, and a strong breeze blew his hair off his forehead. "Is this the spot where they've been filming?"

Duke nodded. "Great view, isn't it?"

"I'll say," Joe said as he stepped up to the wide cement sill and stared down at the grid of city streets far below. "And dangerous, too."

"Where are my extras?" the director shouted.

"Right here," Duke answered as Joe backed away from the window and joined the other extras.

"Okay, guys, here's the deal. We'll start with—" Sachs sized up the three extras, then clapped a hand on Joe's shoulder. "You. What's your name, kid?"

"Joe Hardy."

"Okay, Joe." The director pointed to a rubber

mat that had been laid out like a runway next to the outer wall. "All you have to do is walk on that mat. You'll pass Angelique. She'll be sitting in the corner of the arch here, singing. You'll see her, react right about here—" Sachs walked in between the open arch and the lighting scaffold, stopping in the middle. "You think—dynamite girl! You count to ten—to yourself, of course— then walk on to the end of the mat. Got it?"

Joe gave a thumbs-up sign. "No problem."

"As soon as Joe hits the end of the mat, the next guy will start down the mat and do the same routine. Okay?" Sachs asked.

The other two guys nodded.

"Then let's go," Sachs said. "Contact the copter, tell them we're ready. Places!"

Everybody moved at once. Duke leaned against the light scaffold and spoke into his walkie-talkie, cuing the helicopter. Joe took his place at the end of the mat and waited for his cue. This was fun, he thought, grinning.

Two crew members ran over and ripped the tape off the arched opening. Angelique was escorted to her place at the side of the arched opening farthest from Joe, while the lights clicked on with a low hum. Crew members scrambled around, making last-minute adjustments before ducking out of the camera's view.

"Okay, people, we're rolling tape," the director shouted. "Let's make this one count."

"Copter in place!" Duke shouted.

"Tape rolling!" Someone shouted.

"Give me the audio," Sachs ordered.

Joe saw a woman turn on a large reel-to-reel tape player. There were four loud clicks, then the song began. Angelique swayed in time to the music.

"Cue the extra," Sachs shouted.

Someone gave Joe a nudge, and he started moving slowly along the mat. This is a cinch, he thought. Just act natural, stay cool. And I definitely don't need to pretend that Angelique is dynamite.

Reaching his spot to stop, Joe gazed to his left, toward Angelique. She looked great in a delicately ruffled white blouse that covered the thighs of her sleek black leggings. The breeze blew in from the side of her, tousling her honey blond hair.

"The sidewalks of your mind lead to friends you've left behind," she mouthed along with the track, winking at Joe as he finished counting to ten.

Joe had just started forward again with the open arch on his left when he heard a noise that was definitely not part of the video. A quick glance to the right showed him that the lighting scaffold next to him was wobbling.

"Get back!" Duke shouted, jumping away from the scaffold. A three-foot-wide light was slipping. Before Joe could move, the light swung back, then rotated forward, and hit Joe squarely in the jaw.

Joe grunted as the swinging light sent him

flying. He grappled for balance, his arms flailing as he tumbled onto the cement sill and rolled out of the arch!

His eyes fixed on the city street thousands of feet below him.

He was falling off the building!

Chapter
Twelve

JOE PAWED AT the cement sill, not falling at least, but still without a solid grip on it. His feet were like lead weights as his body hung over the side and dangled in midair.

He had to wrap his fingers around the sill.

Behind him he heard the whir of helicopter rotors as the craft hovered on a level with him. They couldn't help him. If the copter got too close, the wind could send it crashing against the building.

His fingers scraped against the stone, but it was useless. "Ugh," he groaned as his hands started to slip off the smooth surface. This is it, he thought.

Just then something squeezed his wrist and his fall was broken.

"Gotcha!"

Tipping his head back, Joe saw Frank's face,

his jaw tense as he held on to Joe's wrist with all his strength.

"Don't let go!" Joe shouted.

Nancy appeared beside Frank and grabbed Joe's other wrist. "We'll pull you up on the count of three," Nancy shouted. "Try to relax."

"Okay," Joe called up.

"One, two," Frank shouted, "three!"

Joe turned his face away as his body was scraped along the building's facade. A moment later, Nancy and Frank were pulling him over the lip of the sill.

"That was close." Joe collapsed onto the floor, breathing heavily.

"Too close." Nancy gently patted Joe's arm.

"Oh, Joe!" Angelique knelt beside him and touched his forehead. "Are you hurt?"

"I'll be okay," he said, sitting back and taking in the crew that surrounded him.

"I'm so sorry," Angelique said over her shoulder as she was escorted back to the makeup area.

"Thank goodness you're okay," the director said. "Where's the gaffer? Didn't I tell you people that the lighting equipment was too close to the set?" Sachs pulled the lighting director aside and began to argue in hushed tones.

One by one, the crew members returned to their tasks.

Joe stood up and brushed himself off.

"If you ask me, that was a freaky accident," Frank said, glancing over at the scaffold.

"An accident—or foul play?" Nancy asked.

"Let's check it out." Joe, Frank, and Nancy checked the scaffold, where the lighting crew was already on the job.

"I don't get it," said the lighting director. "We use this setup all the time."

Joe took a closer look at the scaffold. Each light was fastened to the rod with round clips held tight by bolts.

"It's a good thing this light wasn't on for that shot," one technician told Joe. "You could have been burned, too." He checked the clamp that held the light to the pipe. "The clip is good. Otherwise it would have fallen to the ground. But the bolts are gone."

Frank and Joe exchanged a look.

"No bolts!" the director fumed. "What am I paying you people for?"

Nancy and Frank and Joe moved away from the group and were joined by Fish.

"I just talked to a friend of mine on the crew," Fish said. "He's never seen anything like that happen before."

"It seems suspicious to me," Nancy said. "I can't believe a technician would be so careless."

"Well," Frank said, "if someone did rig that light to hit Joe, there's a new question. Who would want to finish him off?"

"Someone who wants us off this case," Joe said, taking in everyone on the set. "But who?"

No one had an answer.

* * *

An hour later, as Nancy sat in a cab creeping through rush-hour traffic, she tried to concentrate on the problem of finding Jane's identity.

In the front seat Joe was talking baseball with the driver. Sitting in the backseat between Fish and Frank, Nancy asked them what they'd thought of Angelique's description of Jane.

"I wouldn't take her seriously," Fish said. "The princess doesn't speak well of anyone."

"On the other hand," Frank said, "if what Angelique says is true, it could explain why Jane knows 'My Broken Heart.' Angelique admitted that Jane worked for Crockett at one time. And from what Joe and I saw today, just about anyone can walk into Skyler, Inc. If Jane was bitter enough, she could have swiped the music."

"There's definitely a connection between Jane and the Skylers," Nancy said. "Maybe we'll learn more at Top of the Charts tonight. Ever since I found that matchbook with Jane's belongings, I've been wanting to check that restaurant out."

"You'll like it," Fish said. "It's an old roller rink that was converted to a club about ten years ago. If Jane is in the business, someone there will know her. That place is crawling with singers, producers, musicians, and wannabes. I wish I could join you, but I've got a late session for another artist at the studio."

"We'll also get a chance to keep an eye on Veronica," Joe said, remembering the dinner appointment penciled into the woman's appointment book.

Back at the girls' suite at the Astor Towers, Jane decided that she didn't feel up to a night on the town. She was finishing a dinner sent up by room service when Nancy and Bess said goodbye.

By the time they arrived at Top of the Charts, the Hardys were already seated at a booth on the perimeter of the circular room.

"Scaled any buildings lately?" Bess smiled at Joe as she slid into the booth.

"I guess Nancy told you about my adventure at the top of the Chrysler Building," Joe said, sinking back against the cushion of the banquette.

"She sure did," Bess said. "I'm glad to see that you're okay."

"I just wish we knew whether it was an accident—or a deliberate attack on Joe," Frank said.

Nancy nodded. "With no evidence to go on, it's a tough one to call."

"Look over there. Our waiter's going to sing," Bess said as their handsome waiter rushed up to stand next to the piano. He grabbed a microphone and sang along with the pianist. Nancy scanned the crowd as she listened and noticed Angelique and Veronica sitting at a table across the room, laughing and talking.

She nudged Frank and pointed.

"They were here when we arrived," Joe said, eyeing the two women. "We've been watching them."

"I've been watching them," Frank grumbled. "Joe's been *staring* at them. Would you turn around and quit mooning?"

"You're just jealous," Joe said.

"For someone who's too stressed out to record an album, Angelique's certainly putting up a good front," Nancy observed.

Bess nodded. "Shouldn't she be home, resting her throat?"

"It's only affected by her singing," Joe said, defending her, "not talking."

Frank watched Angelique sign a few autographs and chat with her mother. She certainly didn't appear to have a care in the world. Either she was a great actress, or all the stuff about the embezzlement and her parents didn't really bug her.

"I thought Veronica would be here with Mario," Joe said. He told the girls about the airline tickets to the Cayman Islands he'd found in Veronica's desk.

Frank also explained how they'd found Mario going through Crockett's files.

"So you think Mario and Veronica might be the embezzlers?" Nancy asked.

"They both have motive," Joe pointed out.

"And access to Skyler, Inc.," Frank added.

Their waiter finished his song, then bowed the entire way into the kitchen.

"I love this place," Bess said as another waiter began to perform. "Music, food, and adorable waiters. What more could you want?"

A few minutes later their waiter returned with a huge tray covered with steaming plates. After he served the entrées, Nancy asked him about Jane's photo.

"I don't know her," he said, shaking his head. "Why are you looking for her?"

Not wanting to reveal the details of her case, Nancy concocted a story. "I work for a casting director on Broadway," she told the waiter. "This singer auditioned for a part, and the producer wants her badly. But somehow we lost her résumé."

The waiter's eyes lit up. Like most of the other waiters there, he was an aspiring performer, hoping for a break. A casting director had the power to make things happen for him.

"I wish I could help you," he said, flashing Nancy a big smile. "Let me spread the word to the other servers. Maybe someone can help you find your vocalist." He fished a business card out of his pocket and handed it to Nancy. "And the next time you're casting a male role, give me a call."

"Will do," Nancy said as he hurried off.

"Now you've done it," Frank said. "In two seconds every wannabe will be flocking around you."

"Exactly what I was hoping for," Nancy said, taking a bite of lemon chicken and waiting for the mob.

Before Nancy had finished eating, half a dozen servers had stopped by the table. None of them recognized Jane, but each one gave Nancy a business card, and a few handed her glossy photos of themselves.

As Joe swallowed the last bite of his steak, he listened to another server singing—a jazz tune this time. A chestnut-skinned woman with short-cropped hair, she had a deep, full voice.

When the woman finished her song, she strolled up to Nancy's table. "Roxy Williams," she said, handing Nancy a picture and résumé. "I hear you're casting a female role?"

"Actually, the producer *insists* on hiring this singer." Nancy pointed to Jane's photo.

Roxy focused on the picture and nodded. "Her name's Jane Orbach."

Jane! That explained why the girl's eyes had lit up when Detective Lebowitz had first called her Jane.

"Jane Orbach," Bess repeated, smiling. "I can't wait to tell—"

"The producer," Nancy said, interrupting before Bess blew their story. "Do you know how we can get in touch with her?" she pressed, hoping for an address or phone number.

Roxy shrugged. "She lives on the Upper West Side, I think. She was in my acting class, but I haven't seen her around for a while. Maybe your client would let me read for the part?"

"Sorry," Nancy said. "The producer has his mind made up. But I'll keep your picture, for any future work."

As Roxy left the table, Bess said, "At last we've

learned Jane's real name. Should we head back to the hotel and give her the good news?"

Nancy hesitated. It was nearly ten o'clock, and Jane had been exhausted by the events of the past two days. "Why don't we let her rest? We can tell her in the morning. We should call Detective Lebowitz to let him know, too. If this name checks out and leads us to an address, the police will be able to close Jane's case."

Just then Nancy heard a stir behind her.

"It's Mario," Frank said, peeking over her shoulder. "Now things should heat up."

A murmur swept through the dining room as Mario moved to join Veronica and Angelique. Frank saw that Angelique's happy expression had become angry.

Before he could think any more about it, Frank was interrupted by their waiter wheeling a dessert cart over to them. He and the others ordered five different desserts to share—cakes, pies, and fresh fruit.

"Delicious," Bess said, and she spooned a final raspberry from a crystal bowl.

Nancy was spearing a final bite of fudge cake when she heard a flurry of activity behind her. Whipping around, she saw Angelique throwing a tantrum.

Frank heard Veronica and Angelique arguing heatedly, while Mario remained silent and grinned. "Somehow I'm not surprised," Frank muttered.

Although a waitress was singing at the piano in

the center of the restaurant, all eyes were on Angelique. She stood up, threw her napkin across the table, and marched off toward the rest rooms.

"Let's go see if we can find out what the problem is," Nancy told Bess.

"Good idea," Frank said, still focused on Veronica and Mario, who were paying no attention whatsoever to Angelique's exit. "And I think it's time Joe and I asked Veronica a few questions."

When Frank and Joe approached her, Veronica smiled. "At last, the detectives are here. Sit down," she said coolly.

Mario's black eyes were flat and emotionless. "When I saw you across the room, I knew you'd try to interrogate us before the evening ended."

Frank nudged his brother. "We must be losing our touch if people can guess our next move."

"We've been playing a little game at our table," Joe said. "You know 'Name That Tune'? Well, how about naming the girl in this photo?"

"A pretty girl," Mario observed, "though I can't tell you her name.

Veronica studied the photo for a moment, then shrugged. "I've never met her."

"Angelique knows her," Joe prodded.

"Oh, really?" Veronica shrugged. "Let's get to the point. What can I tell you that would help solve your case?" she asked, pushing a lock of dark hair behind an ear studded with a single diamond.

"You could lead us to the missing two million dollars," Joe said lightly.

Veronica laughed. "If I knew where the money was, I wouldn't be here now."

"Where would you be?" Frank probed. "Somewhere in the Caribbean? The Cayman Islands?"

Veronica's dark eyes opened wide in surprise. "So you know about our vacation?" she said, slipping her hand into Mario's. "You may be better detectives than I thought."

"You're way off track," Mario said. "You're focusing on the victims when you *should* be investigating the man who hired you."

"Crockett?" Joe said.

Mario nodded. "He's the thief. He cheated me. Now he's robbing his own daughter and Veronica blind." He raised his index finger in a warning gesture. "He'll get you, too."

Nancy and Bess found Angelique sitting on the counter in the powder room, sobbing.

Nancy pulled out a chair and sat down close to Angelique. "Are you okay?"

Angelique lifted her head, and Nancy noticed that her eyes were red and puffy. "Oh, Nancy," she wailed, "I'm being torn apart. I'm losing my mother to that creep Mario. She totally ignores me when he's around, and I won't take it anymore!" She bowed her head as a fresh wave of tears washed down her cheeks.

"Don't worry," Bess said, and patted the girl on the back.

"Then there's my father. He doesn't care about me. Not really. I'm just a toy, a pretty little doll who will make him rich."

Nancy and Bess weren't sure what to say to the distraught girl.

"But you have millions of fans who adore you," Bess said gently.

"They don't know me," Angelique snapped. "No one knows the real me. No one cares." She wiped the tears from her face and jumped off the counter. "I'm sick and tired of being 'their' star."

Her brown eyes sparkled with fresh tears as she added, "Maybe it's time for this star to fall out of the sky." She spun around and stormed out of the ladies' room, leaving Nancy and Bess to wonder about her cryptic remark.

Outside, she marched right past Joe, who was hoping for the chance to cheer her up.

"Angelique—wait up," he called after her.

She never looked back.

Maybe I'm losing my touch, Joe thought, straightening up and returning to the table.

"I can't believe it's after midnight." Bess yawned as she followed Nancy into an elevator back at the Astor Towers. "The waiters at Top of the Charts are great entertainers. I could have stayed all night."

"Good thing you don't have a rehearsal for 'Rising Star' tomorrow," Nancy said. "You have a day off, though we have a few things to take care of in the morning. We should call Detective

Lebowitz. Now that we know Jane's name, we need to find out where she lives. Hey! She might even be listed in the phone book."

After the elevator arrived on their floor, the girls moved quickly down the corridor. "Jane's probably asleep," Nancy said, quietly sticking the key into the door leading into the living room. The girls had agreed that Jane could use the smaller bedroom, while Nancy and Bess would share the other.

"Hit the lights, I can't see," Bess whispered.

Reaching inside the door, Nancy flicked on the lights, then went to sit on the couch while she pulled off her shoes. Bess had tiptoed into their bedroom when Nancy heard a low, muffled noise. It sounded like whimpering, and it was coming from Jane's bedroom.

Poor Jane, Nancy thought, silently crossing to the door of the girl's room. She must be having a nightmare.

She cracked the door and peered inside. The room was dark, and Nancy couldn't see a thing. Then all at once the cries sounded desperate. Something was wrong.

Nancy fumbled for the light switch and flicked it on—but nothing happened. Then she flung the door wide open, and a shaft of light streamed inside and landed on the bed.

The light hit the figure of a man, bent over the bed. He was crouched there, holding a pillow over a rumpled mass of bed sheets.

He was smothering Jane!

Chapter

Thirteen

N<small>ANCY COULD NOW</small> make out Jane flailing and kicking under the sheets, struggling to free herself from the man who was too strong for her.

"Stop!" Nancy shouted.

The man lifted an arm to shield his eyes from the light. His face was obscured by a black ski mask, and his hair was covered by a black baseball cap.

Desperate to stop him, Nancy aimed a karate kick at the attacker's upper body.

He leapt aside at the last second. Nancy spun around to kick again, but the man had already scuttled past her and out the door.

Hoping to identify the man by his build at least, Nancy chased him out to the well-lit corridor. She caught only a flash of muscular arms and shoulders under a black T-shirt before he ducked through the emergency exit and thundered down the stairs.

With no hope of catching him, Nancy returned to the suite, where she found Jane sitting up on one of the sofas in the living room. She was sobbing in Bess's arms.

"Are you all right?" Nancy asked.

Jane nodded.

"I called the front desk," Bess said.

"Fast thinking," Nancy said. "With luck, the hotel's security team can catch the attacker before he leaves the building."

Ten minutes later Jane had calmed down enough to discuss the attack with Nancy, Bess, and a hotel security guard named Dole.

"I'm glad you called us as soon as you did," the silver-haired guard told the girls. "My people checked all the exits, but he seems to have slipped away."

"I wish I could be more helpful," Jane said, "but I never saw his face. How do you think he got in?" she asked, her eyes wide with fear. "I'm sure the door was locked when I went to sleep."

"He picked the lock," Nancy answered. She had already checked out the door leading into the suite. "I was so tired, I didn't notice the damage when Bess and I came in, but apparently he had some trouble with the lock." She pointed to the door to the hallway. Mr. Dole went over and opened it.

"Yes, he nearly botched it," Dole agreed. "The chrome around the lock is scraped."

"The man is obviously not experienced," Nancy said, "though he did think some things through." She explained that when she'd flicked the light switch, nothing had happened in the bedroom. "The attacker unscrewed all the light bulbs in your room, Jane. Also, his face was masked by the stocking cap," she said thoughtfully.

Dole pulled at his mustache thoughtfully. "Well, then, this wasn't a burglary attempt."

Nancy looked at Jane, who sat on the sofa wrapped in Bess's terry-cloth robe, then nodded. "It does seem that the intruder was after Jane."

Jane shuddered and brushed her dark hair off her forehead with resolve. "At least now I know I'm not crazy. All those feelings I've had of impending danger have some basis in reality."

"I can't let you stay in this suite," Dole said, picking up the phone. "For your own safety, we'll move you to another suite. Don't give anyone the number of the new suite."

As she packed her clothes, Nancy made a mental list of everyone who knew where the girls were staying. She'd been careful not to give out any information at Top of the Charts. The Hardys, of course, had seen the suite. Fish knew where they were—and she had given the exact suite number to Angelique.

There had to be some connection between Jane and Angelique, something that Nancy hadn't uncovered as yet. She was glad that the Hardys had borrowed Jane's picture to show Crockett. Maybe he could help solve the puzzle.

Thirty minutes later, with the help of Mr. Dole and one of the bellboys, the girls had moved their belongings to the Presidential Suite.

"Wow!" Bess said when Mr. Dole showed them around the deluxe suite of rooms, which included a kitchen, a dining room with a huge conference table, a stereo, and a grand piano in the sitting room. "All the comforts of home," Bess said.

"If you live in a palace," Nancy teased.

Bess ran her hand over the piano. "This will come in handy when I practice tomorrow."

"This suite has its own security system," Dole explained, showing them a small box mounted on the wall by the door.

"How does it work?" Nancy asked.

"If someone tampers with the locks, a silent alarm goes off at the main desk. You can rest assured that no one will bother you tonight. I'll file my report with the police and bid you good night, ladies." Dole retreated to the door.

Although she was tired, Nancy had one more thing to take care of before she went to bed. While she searched the suite for a phone book, she remembered to tell Jane that Roxy had identified her photograph.

"Jane Orbach." The dark-haired girl nodded, then smiled. "That explains why I felt so comfortable being called Jane—it's my name!"

Bess laughed. "I'm glad you're being such a good sport about all this."

Jane said, "It's you two who are the good sports. If it weren't for you, I'd be in the hospital still or in a shelter." She smiled gratefully at Nancy.

Nancy smiled back and began leafing through the phone book. She ran her finger down a column of names until she came to Orbach, Jane. "Here you are—on West Seventy-first Street."

"No kidding?" Jane read over her shoulder.

"We'll check out this address in the morning," Nancy promised.

"That's great," Bess said. "If Roxy is right, you might be home tomorrow."

Jane shuddered. "That's pretty scary after what happened tonight."

Nancy agreed, and knew there was no way she could abandon Jane with a potential murderer on the loose.

Early Wednesday morning the Hardys stopped at a deli for bagels before heading straight for Crockett's office in the Brill Building. Frank planned to spend the morning sifting through Skyler, Inc.'s business files for clues to the missing money.

"There's nothing like a New York bagel," Joe said, biting into an onion bagel slathered with cream cheese as he sat in Crockett's office.

"I wish you were as interested in these files as

you are in breakfast," Frank complained, pulling an armload of folders out of a drawer.

"Paperwork's a drag," Joe said, "especially when we could be watching Angelique tape another segment of her video just a few blocks away."

Frank pushed a pile of demo tapes to one side of Crockett's desk and opened a folder. The producer was off at the video shoot, though his secretary knew that Frank and Joe had total access to the company's files.

As Frank leafed through the file, he noticed that each document had the same heading: American Federation of Musicians—Recording Contract. "Check it out. Contracts between Skyler, Inc., and its various musicians. We should skim these."

Joe glanced at the pile of documents and winced. "There must be a hundred."

"What do you expect from a producer like Crockett?" Frank divided the stack of contracts and handed half to his brother. "Think you can squeeze these into your busy schedule?"

"This is it," Nancy said as the cab pulled up in front of a brick apartment building on West Seventy-first Street. The four-story building was on a narrow street lined with shady green trees.

"Nice neighborhood," Bess said, climbing out of the cab. She stared up at the building, then studied Jane's face for a reaction. "What do *you* think? Does it feel like home?"

"Yes, it does," Jane admitted, though she didn't seem happy about it. "But it makes me nervous." She held her hands to her chest, then took a deep breath.

"What's wrong?" Nancy asked.

"I know it sounds silly," Jane said, "but my heart is racing. I'm afraid I'm not safe here."

Nancy studied the tidy building and frowned. "Let's take this one step at a time. When I phoned Lebowitz this morning, he agreed to meet us here. There's no reason we can't go on in. If we don't like the way things look, we'll back off and wait for him out here."

Inside the vestibule, the girls found Jane's name listed beside apartment 3-D. Bess tried to push open the inner door, but it was locked.

"Try the superintendent," Nancy told her. "We need to ask some questions anyway."

Bess pushed the button for the apartment manager, but again there was no answer. "Now what?"

Nancy shrugged. "We'll try them all," she said, running her hand over the buttons.

A moment later the lock buzzed and Bess pushed the inner door open.

The building was quiet as the girls climbed the narrow staircase to the third floor. Nancy had hoped to run into some of Jane's neighbors, but she reminded herself that it was Wednesday morning, and most people would be at work.

When Nancy first spotted apartment 3-D, she noticed the door was battered and pockmarked.

"Why is the door to Jane's apartment all beat up?" Bess asked.

"Looks like someone tried to break in," Nancy said. She went up to the door to investigate. Her stomach flipped over as she realized that only one weapon could have caused that damage. A gun. "These are bullet holes."

"It happened here," Jane gasped. "This is where I heard the gunshots. A man was out in the hall trying to get inside, and he started shooting at my door!"

Nancy squeezed Jane's hand as she examined the lock. Jane's attacker had destroyed it. Nancy turned the knob and pushed, but the door didn't budge.

Just then Nancy heard an almost silent click behind her and felt a solid object being jabbed into her back. She whirled around—and gasped.

She was staring down at the shiny barrel of a .38 caliber revolver.

Her heart hammered in her chest as she raised her eyes from the gun to the beady eyes of the gunman.

"Touch that door again and you're dead."

Chapter

Fourteen

"DON'T WORRY," Nancy said, struggling to keep her voice steady. "I won't even move."

"And put your hands up—all of you," the man growled, swinging the handgun toward Bess and Jane.

"O-Okay." Bess's hands quivered as she lifted them in the air.

Jane's face was white with fear. "It's happening again!" she whimpered, lifting her arms and backing away from the man.

Nancy eyed the bearded man with thinning black hair and broad shoulders. Although they were three against one, he wouldn't be easy to overcome because he was holding a gun.

The man's scowl started to fade when he took a closer look at Jane. "You," he said, staring at her. "So you didn't skip town." He lowered the revolver. "After the shooting that went on here Monday, I've gotten a little overly cautious."

The girls relaxed their arms and lowered them. Nancy was relieved that the man was no longer holding them at gunpoint, but she still didn't trust him.

"Do you live in this building?" Bess asked.

"Upstairs," he answered. "I'm the superintendent *and* the landlord, Tony Caruso."

Nancy introduced herself and Bess, adding, "We're Jane's friends. Can you let us into her apartment?"

Tony pulled a key ring off his belt and opened the door. "I had a new lock installed after your friend shot his way in here. Must have been an ugly scene."

"So you know that a man did this. Did you see him?" Nancy asked.

"I was out at the time." He held the door open with one hand and pointed at Jane with the other. "You'll be charged for the lock. You might want to think about moving out of here. I've had a lot of complaints."

"What about the police?" Nancy asked. "Were they notified about the break-in?"

"Break-in?" Tony scoffed. "I'm guessing it was a boyfriend. Not a break-in. You two have a little fight?"

Jane's face was blank. "I don't—"

"She doesn't want to talk about it right now," Nancy interrupted. "Thanks for your help," she said dismissively.

Tony handed Jane a key, then folded his arms. "Yeah, sure."

Nancy led the way into the apartment, then firmly shut the door behind all three of them. With its red-brick walls and dark hardwood floors covered with hooked rugs, the place was cozy.

"So this is home." Jane circled the room, pausing to touch a vase of dried flowers and a stained-glass lamp. "I remember I found this lamp on the street," she said. "I remember living here. I think I liked this place. . . ." She paused when her eyes locked on the battered door. "Until the man with the gun came after me."

Nancy moved to the center of the room and leaned against the back of a sofa. "Can you remember anything more from that day?" she asked. "Did the man finally leave? How did you manage to escape from him?"

Jane concentrated as she paced past the small white kitchen area to a low, wide windowsill with leafy plants scattered around it. She stared outside for a moment, then snapped her fingers. "I climbed out this window and down that fire escape!"

Joining her at the window, Nancy noticed that the plants had been pushed to one side. "You cleared off the windowsill so that you could climb out."

"That would explain why you didn't have your purse or keys or any ID," Bess said. "You left in a hurry and had to make do with the money in your pockets."

"Wow." Jane rubbed her temples, then sighed. "It's still scary, but I'm starting to feel better. Things are beginning to fall into place."

"Take a close look around the apartment," Nancy suggested. "I'm sure you'll see more things that will jog your memory."

The girls found Jane's purse hanging on a rack by the door. Her wallet was there, with more than a hundred dollars in cash, three credit cards, and her driver's license. "It's a lousy photo," Jane said, staring at the driver's license, "but it's definitely me."

A small pine desk sat against the wall opposite the windows. Jane sat down behind it and ran her hand over the smooth wood.

"This is where I work. I used to sit here for hours—writing, I think." She studied the desktop, which was bare except for a coffee mug stuffed with pencils and pens. "Something's missing."

In the top drawer the girls found an envelope stuffed with cash, which Bess counted quickly. "More than three thousand dollars!"

"It's clear that the man with the gun wasn't robbing you," Nancy said. "Money definitely wasn't the motive."

"But he took something," Jane said, staring at the desk. "Something's missing. There's no paper here—nothing to write on."

It was true. The girls found a sealed packet of

notepads in the bottom drawer, but no scraps of paper anywhere. Nancy was about to close the drawer when she noticed the lines on the paper. "This is music paper—the kind songwriters and composers use."

"That's it!" A smile lit Jane's face. "I'm not a poet. I write songs—and 'Gun-shy' is a song that I was working on. I must have jotted down those lyrics when I thought them up on the Circle Line boat."

"That's why you have this, too," Bess said, pointing to an electric keyboard that was stowed under the desk.

"Right!" Jane clapped her hands together.

Nancy was slipping the bottom drawer of the desk back when she heard a crackling noise. "Sounds like something's back behind this drawer." She slid the drawer out and reached in to pull out a crumpled sheet of hand-scored sheet music.

Bess took the page and began to read the lyrics aloud. " 'Words are all I have for you—' "

"Words won't make your dreams come true," Jane interrupted, her brown eyes sparkling. "My music is coming back to me. At last, the pieces are falling into place!"

"What do you make of this?" Joe pulled a contract out of the stack and handed it to his brother. "It's a deal between Skyler, Inc., and Jane Orbach."

"Interesting," Frank said, scanning the document. "According to this, she recorded four untitled songs for Crockett and was paid a thousand dollars. Not enough to make her rich."

"But it confirms what Angelique told us about Jane," Joe said. "This contract's two years old."

Frank nodded. "I'm going to make a copy of it. Nancy will probably want to see it." He left Crockett's office and made a copy on the machine at the end of the hall. When he returned, he met Crockett outside his office.

"Frank Hardy—just the man I want to see." Crockett smiled and swept his Stetson off his bald head. "Let's step inside. I've got something I need to say to you."

Snapping to attention when he spotted Crockett, Joe stood up and shoved papers back into a folder.

After Crockett walked around to sit in his chair, Frank took Jane's photo out of his pocket and handed it to him. "First, we have a question. We were wondering about this musician you hired two years ago. Jane Orbach. Do you remember her?"

Crockett frowned. "Just barely. Why?"

Frank glanced over at Joe, who nodded. "To make a long story short, we ran into her the other day and she was performing 'My Broken Heart.' She claims to have written the song."

"If that doesn't take the cake!" Crockett slammed his hand on his desk in a burst of anger. "Stealing my daughter's material. She's got to be stopped. Do you know how I can reach her?"

Joe shrugged, and Frank refused to give out

any information that might botch Nancy's case. Finally he answered, "I really couldn't say, but I'll get on it for you."

"No need," Crockett said abruptly. "I appreciate everything you boys have done, but this is what I came here to tell you. I'm afraid we've reached the end of the road. This morning I received a call from the federal investigator who's been looking into the missing funds. He tells me the case is about to break."

Joe scratched his head, wondering if he had understood what the man was saying.

"Thanks, boys." Crockett stood up and patted them each on the back. "It's been a pleasure."

"Wait a minute," Frank said. "Are you telling us that we're off this case?"

Crockett smiled, his eyes gleaming. "No hard feelings, but from this moment on you're fired."

Chapter

Fifteen

FIRED! Frank saw that Joe seemed to be just as surprised by Crockett's announcement as he was.

"We're just starting to make progress," Frank told the producer. He hated to leave a case unfinished. "If you give us a few more days—"

"I'm under strict orders. The G-men are afraid you boys might tip off a key suspect and send the person running."

"I can't believe it," Frank said, deflated. "We haven't crossed paths with a single agent on the case. How did they figure it out?"

Crockett touched an index finger to his lips, indicating that he couldn't talk. "The feds don't want me to discuss the case with anyone." Then he added in a low voice, "They're about to nab the criminals even as we speak."

"Really?" Joe was intrigued. "Who do they think took the money? Veronica and Mario?"

"Boys—please." Crockett looped his thumbs through his belt loops and rocked back on his boot heels. "I've already said too much. Thanks for trying. Have a nice trip back to Bayport."

"Do you recognize the other girl in this picture?" Bess held up a framed photograph that she'd found on the dresser in Jane's bedroom. In the picture Jane was sitting on a bench beside a brunette girl who was holding up a huge pretzel.

"That's my sister," Jane said, taking the photograph from Bess. Her eyes were unfocused, as if her mind were far away. "She's the only family I have since my parents died. My sister and I are very close." She handed the framed photo to Nancy.

"This is great," Bess said. "Being here is bringing back your memory."

"It's true," Jane said happily. She rushed to the dresser, pulled out a drawer, and riffled through the contents. "There must be something here—some key that will bring it all back to me." She moved from the dresser and yanked open the closet.

Glad to see Jane come alive, Nancy glanced back at the photo and noticed a sign in the background. "Check this out," she said, pointing to the tiny print that said Circle Line. "Apparently Monday was not the first time you went on a Circle Line cruise."

"I've been thinking about that," Jane said. "I know I was running from the man with the gun. I also remember that boat rides were one of my favorite ways to unwind. Maybe I jumped on the boat to get away from him and buy some time." Jane glanced back at the photo, then sighed. "I should call my sister to let her know what's happened. If I could just remember her name . . ."

"Why don't you look in your address book, under *O?*" Nancy suggested, remembering the slim address book the girls had found in Jane's purse.

"Good idea." Jane went to her purse, leafed through the book, and nodded. "Sarah Orbach— that's it. I hope she's home," she said, picking up the bedroom phone.

"Let me talk with her when you're finished," Nancy told Jane as she and Bess returned to the living room.

While Jane spoke on the phone, Nancy paced the living room, trying to piece together what she knew about Jane's life. She was a talented singer. From the scrap of lyrics in her pocket and the sheet of hand-scored music, it seemed that Jane was a songwriter, too.

It was also clear that someone was trying to kill her. The intruder who had tried to smother Jane the night before had meant business. The bullet holes in the door were a grim reminder that Jane wasn't safe—especially in this apartment.

Just then the intercom beeped. "That's probably Detective Lebowitz," Nancy said, pushing the door buzzer.

"Someone's been doing a little target practice," the detective said a minute later at Jane's door after seeing the bullet holes. "The good news is that it looks like he left us some rounds to examine."

Evidence. Nancy watched as the detective opened his briefcase and removed a plastic bag and a pair of tweezers. Within minutes he had plucked two metal slugs from the door.

"The landlord told us the shooting occurred on Monday, the same day that Jane ended up on the Circle Line boat," Nancy told the detective.

"Is that right?" he said thoughtfully.

"Can you tell what kind of gun the bullets came from?" Nancy asked.

"I'll send them to the lab for an analysis," Lebowitz said. "But from experience, I'd say the gun was a .38 caliber."

Just like Tony the landlord's gun, Nancy thought. "In that case," she said, "you should know that the owner of this building has a revolver, and it looked to me like a thirty-eight." She told the detective how the girls had been greeted.

"Tony Caruso, huh?" Lebowitz scribbled the name on a notepad. "I'll run a check on him."

"Will you be able to tell if the bullets in this door came from his gun?" Nancy asked.

"I'll need to bring the gun to the lab. I can ask to see his permit, but unless he offers me the gun, I'll have to wait for a warrant," the detective explained.

Bess spun around from the bookcase, where she'd been checking out Jane's collection of books. "Do you really think Tony Caruso is the man who's trying to kill Jane?"

Nancy waited a minute for the detective to answer, then said, "It's possible. Something about that guy gives me the creeps."

Lebowitz nodded. "It's worth checking out, though I don't know why Jane's landlord would want to attack her, unless she's behind on the rent."

"That's probably not the case." Bess told the detective about the sizable amount of cash that the girls had found in Jane's apartment.

"Then we're definitely not talking about robbery," Detective Lebowitz said, scratching his chin. "Though considering the patrol officer's report on your uninvited guest last night, I'm not surprised." He leafed through the papers on his clipboard until he found the report. "Attempted homicide. You girls had an exciting evening."

"We're just worried that the man will come after Jane again," Bess said.

"Then it would be wise for Jane to stay with you in the Presidential Suite at the Astor," Lebowitz said. "That place has high-tech security, rigged for diplomats and visiting heads of state."

Detective Lebowitz headed for the door. "I'm going to do a sweep of the apartments in this building," he said. "Someone had to be around when the door was shot up. Gunfire is not the kind of thing you forget."

As the front door closed, Jane appeared in the bedroom doorway and motioned Nancy to come to the phone. "My sister wants to fly here right away," Jane said, holding her hand over the mouthpiece. "Please tell her it's not necessary. She's in a summer stock theater—it's an opportunity she shouldn't miss."

Nancy spoke briefly with Jane's sister, who seemed startled by the events Jane had described to her. Nancy questioned her about Jane's profession, but Sarah only knew that Jane was involved in the music industry. She said that Jane had never given her any details. Nancy was a little frustrated but kept it to herself.

"Jane's in good hands," Nancy reassured the concerned woman on the phone. "Why don't you fly out after your season ends?"

Once Sarah was reassured, Nancy hung up and returned to the living room, where Detective Lebowitz was lingering by the door.

"Aside from a cleaning lady who comes on Wednesdays, the building is deserted. I don't have any info on your gunman, but I'll check at the precinct to see if a report was filed."

"We'll call your office tomorrow to check in," Nancy promised as the detective left.

An hour later the girls had made an inventory

of Jane's apartment and Jane had packed a small bag to take with her to the Astor Towers.

"Let's take this with us," Nancy said, handing Jane the single page of sheet music.

Jane tucked the page into her bag, along with a blank pad of staff paper she'd taken out of the desk. "I'm glad to have my purse and my own clothes. Though it was nice of you two to lend me some of yours."

"I just wish we'd been able to learn something about the man who chased you out of here," Nancy said, gazing out at the fire escape that zigzagged down to the back alley.

"We'd better get going. We're supposed to meet Frank and Joe at our hotel for lunch," Bess said.

When they reached the first-floor vestibule, Nancy noticed a row of mailboxes across from the intercom system. "Why don't you check your mailbox?" she suggested. "There might be a letter or postcard that will help us piece things together."

Inside her purse Jane found a key ring and opened the mailbox. Magazines and fliers burst out.

Bess picked up the magazines and dusted them off. *"Billboard* and *Rolling Stone.* You're definitely in the music business."

Jane smiled. "I'm beginning to feel like a real person again. Here's a phone bill, an electric bill, and—a personal letter." She tore it open, read the note, and gasped. Her lower lip began to tremble as her hands went limp and the note fluttered to the floor.

"What's wrong?" Nancy asked, bending to pick up the note.

The hand-printed message was simple: Stop acting crazy, or you will sing your last tune.

Chapter

Sixteen

O<small>H NO</small>!" Jane's composure was shattered and she backed into a corner of the vestibule. "It's the man who tried to kill me. He's closing in."

"It's okay," Nancy said, touching the girl's arm gently. "He's not here now, and he's *not* going to get close to you."

"That's an odd threat," Bess said. "I wonder what he means by 'Stop acting crazy'?"

"We'd better show this to Detective Lebowitz," Nancy said, frowning. "We'll drop it by the precinct on our way back to the hotel." Deep down she knew that not even New York's Finest could trace a plain white envelope with a New York City postmark.

"I don't know how much more of this I can take," Jane whispered. She appeared to be washed out and ready to faint.

"Come on," Nancy said, taking the young woman by the arm. "Let's get out of here."

The burst of fresh air helped for only a moment. At the bottom of the steps, Tony Caruso stood on the sidewalk, blocking their path.

"I've been waiting for you girls," he said as he angrily dragged a broom across the pavement. "You put the cops onto me, and I don't like it."

Bess and Jane froze, but Nancy pressed on, easing Jane down the steps beside her.

"We just answered a few questions—*honestly,*" Nancy said, smiling sweetly.

"Yeah, well, I don't like cops in my building." Caruso pointed his broomstick at Jane and shook it menacingly. "I warned you before—I want you out of my building. Get your stuff out of that apartment by the end of the week."

"That's ridiculous," Jane said, suddenly spurred to anger.

"You can't do that," Nancy said. "She must have a lease."

"If she does"—Caruso leaned on his broom and smiled smugly—"*I* don't have a copy of it."

Turning away from him, Nancy made a mental note to check for the lease the next time she came. They had to find it or else Jane would lose her apartment.

The Hardys decided to walk the dozen blocks from the Brill Building to the Astor Towers.

As Frank turned up Fifth Avenue, he couldn't

stop mulling over the case. "There's something weird going on here. Wouldn't it be wild if the embezzler was right under our noses?"

Joe lifted his sunglasses to eye his brother. "I take it this means we're still on the case?"

"You got it," Frank said. "We know that Jane worked for Crockett. We found the contract. Angelique called Jane a troublemaker—"

"I see where you're going," Joe said. "And we know Jane stole Angelique's material. We heard it ourselves."

"Exactly." Frank paused in front of the brass and glass revolving door to the Astor Towers. "And Jane *claims* to have amnesia, but what if it's all a hoax? What if she's scamming Nancy and Bess? Maybe Jane is the embezzler, and her amnesia is all a cover-up."

"We'd better fill Nancy in," Joe said, pushing on the door, "before it's too late."

The Hardys were halfway across the marble floor of the lobby when they heard Nancy call out to them. "Frank! Joe! Over here."

Spinning around, Frank spotted Nancy waving at them from a small elevator bank manned by a security guard. The guys joined her.

"We were just on our way to your suite," Frank explained. "What's up?"

"I wanted to catch you before you went up," Nancy said. "We've moved to the Presidential Suite."

"No kidding!" Joe exclaimed, pushing his sunglasses up on his head. "Did 'Rising Star' give you an upgrade?"

"It's a little more complicated than that," Nancy said, waiting while the guys signed their names in the book at the security desk beside the elevator. "I'll explain it all while we ride up. Bess just ordered a platter of sandwiches from room service."

As the elevator whirred up to the penthouse, Nancy told the guys about the intruder who had attacked Jane the night before. Then she described the bullet holes in the door of Jane's apartment and the surly landlord who had held them at gunpoint. "And as if that wasn't bad enough, when we stopped to check Jane's mail on the way out, she found a threatening letter. And I quote: 'Stop acting crazy, or you will sing your last tune.'"

Joe whistled. "Not exactly fan mail, is it?"

Despite everything he'd heard, Frank still wasn't convinced of Jane's innocence. As they stepped off the elevator, he touched Nancy's arm, motioning her to hang back for a moment.

"I know it looks like someone's trying to kill Jane," Frank said in a low voice. "But have you considered the possibility that she might be involved in some sort of crime—like the embezzling at Skyler, Inc.?"

Frank showed Nancy the contract they'd found between Jane and Skyler, Inc. "We know she once did some work for Crockett," he said.

"But the worst was when we told Crockett about Jane singing 'My Broken Heart,'" Joe added. "He blew his stack. Said something about Jane stealing Angelique's material."

"An angry producer is the *last* thing Jane needs right now," Nancy said.

"Sorry," Frank apologized. "We didn't let on that we knew where he could find her. But it made me start wondering if we should trust Jane. Maybe her memory loss is an act to throw us off the track."

Nancy frowned thoughtfully. "I did consider that. Jane seems sincere, but I admit, I'm a little uneasy about the blank spaces—all the things she doesn't remember."

"I'd hate to see her cause you and Bess trouble," Frank told Nancy. "Be careful."

"Don't worry about me. I've got you to back me up," Nancy said, smiling as she punched the code into the keypad and opened the door to their suite.

Stepping inside Frank heard piano music and then saw the baby grand in the center of the living room. Jane and Bess were sitting on the piano bench as Jane played and sang a song.

"A piano—and a stereo system," Joe said, checking out the girls' new suite. "Some people have all the luck."

"Hi, guys," Bess called over the music. "Listen to this. It's another song Jane wrote. We found one page of the music in her apartment, but she was able to remember the rest."

"Words are all I have for you. Words can't make your dreams come true," Jane sang.

Sinking into an armchair, Frank closed his eyes and concentrated on the song. The melody and lyrics were hauntingly familiar.

"Like it?" Bess asked. "It's called 'Words.'"

"Words!" Frank bolted upright in the chair and nudged his brother. "Sound familiar?"

Joe turned away from the stereo and listened to the song. Then he groaned. "Not again."

"It's one of Angelique's songs—from the unreleased album," Frank said.

Alarmed, Jane stopped playing. "How do you know?"

"We heard a tape of the rough mix in Crockett's office," Joe explained.

"I give up!" Harsh notes filled the air as Jane banged her hands on the piano. "Maybe I should just introduce myself to Angelique and let *her* explain everything," Jane said.

"I'm not sure that's a good idea," Nancy said, then explained that Crockett had accused Jane of stealing his daughter's material.

"Great," Jane muttered, standing up and walking to the window. "Someone's trying to kill me. Crockett's probably going to take me to court. My landlord's threatening to throw me out of my apartment. And my entire life is a blur. Considering what I *do* know, maybe the rest isn't worth remembering!"

Her shoulders shook and she started to sob. Nancy and Bess rushed over to her to try to calm her.

Joe stared glumly at Frank, then switched on the stereo and collapsed in a chair.

After a few minutes the three girls rejoined the guys. Jane gave them a weak smile and said, "Sorry. This amnesia is really overwhelming sometimes."

Joe and Frank smiled back at her, then Frank filled the girls in on Crockett's decision to take them off the case.

"But you're still coming to Saturday's taping of 'Rising Star,' aren't you?" Bess asked, alarmed.

"And we can definitely use your help in trying to piece Jane's memory back," Nancy added as she tossed a strand of reddish blond hair back over her shoulder. And in keeping her safe, she silently added.

"We're glad to stay. How could we miss Bess's national TV debut?" Frank said. And find out whether Jane is a victim or a criminal, he thought.

Just then the door buzzed and a waiter wheeled in a cart with sandwiches and drinks.

"What do we do about that appointment we made with Thornberg for this afternoon?" Joe asked as he plucked a tuna sandwich from the platter.

Frank sipped a cola as he considered their appointment with the federal agent assigned to Crockett's case. "Let's keep it, just to follow up. I want to know who the feds are planning to arrest.

And a few hints from Thornberg might help us clear Jane of wrongdoing."

After lunch the girls planned to check out Greenwich Village, then return to the suite so Bess could rehearse for "Rising Star."

"We'll meet you back here around six o'clock," Nancy said.

The guys said goodbye, then took a cab to Thornberg's office in a skyscraper near City Hall.

After a brief wait, a receptionist showed them into an office overlooking Foley Square. Behind the desk sat a man in his forties with salt-and-pepper hair. He stood and straightened his tie when the boys walked in. "Paul Thornberg. And you must be Fenton Hardy's boys."

"I'm Frank, and this is my brother, Joe," Frank said as he shook the man's hand.

"Please sit down." Thornberg propped reading glasses on his nose and opened a folder. "We have some interesting developments to discuss."

"So we heard," Joe said, leaning forward to speak confidentially. "Who are you arresting?"

Thornberg pulled off his glasses and stared at Joe. "The case hasn't gone *that* far."

"Are you closing in on suspects?" Frank said.

"No, not yet," Thornberg answered. "But that suspicion you had about the Cayman Islands panned out. I called in a favor from a federal agent buddy of mine. He's a master on computers and knows how to access information in the Cayman Islands' banking system without being detected. He traced the stolen funds to a bank account code-named PIKA that's been set up there."

Adrenaline made Frank's heart race. "So who stole the money?"

"The account is a trust fund, set up for a woman named"—Thornberg stuck his glasses back on and read—"Jane Orbach."

Chapter

Seventeen

JANE?" Joe looked as if he had just been forced to swallow vinegar.

Frank sighed and slid back in his chair. He usually loved it when a case came together. However, this was one time he wasn't happy that his suspicions had been proven.

"Do you know this individual?" the agent asked.

"Yes, we're acquainted with her." Frank told Thornberg that Jane was an amnesia victim. "A friend of ours—another detective—is trying to help Jane piece her life together."

"I see," Thornberg said thoughtfully.

"Are you going to charge her with the embezzlement?" Joe asked.

"Not yet," the older man answered. "It's on my schedule to question her, though I don't know how reliable her answers will be if she's just suffered a head injury."

Something isn't making sense here, Frank thought, scratching his head. "Crockett must have gotten mixed up when you told him about Jane Orbach," he said to Thornberg. "He seems to think that the embezzlement case is almost solved."

"Crockett Skyler doesn't know about Ms. Orbach—or the secret account," Thornberg said sternly. "I haven't spoken to the man in days, and I trust you boys will keep this news quiet."

So Crockett lied to us, Frank thought. Why? The case seemed as rocky as a cruise through a hurricane.

"Now that you know about the secret account, is Jane Orbach a prime suspect?" Joe asked.

"Not really," the agent said. "We're still examining Veronica Skyler and her boyfriend, and we've questioned the accountant a few times. We've verified the tip you gave us about Veronica and Mario's flight to the Cayman Islands. I have to warn you not to press them. We can't have them fleeing the country before we can build a case."

"We'll stay away from Veronica and Mario," Frank agreed. "But I don't understand why you're holding back on arresting Jane Orbach. Especially now that you know the account is in her name."

"Although the money is in trust for Ms.

Orbach, the account isn't proof that she was involved in the theft of the funds. She might not even know that the account exists. A trust account in a foreign bank can be opened with a minimum of information and fuss."

Suddenly Frank saw the case in a new light. If Jane was involved, there had to be someone working with her—perhaps the man who had attacked her in the girls' hotel suite.

Maybe Jane and her partner had argued over the money. Maybe their fight had caused her to flee from her apartment and run onto the Circle Line. The question was, who was Jane Orbach's accomplice?

"I wish we had more time to shop," Bess said as the girls drifted into a flea market that had been set up in a Greenwich Village school yard.

Everywhere Nancy looked she saw the brilliant colors of summer. There were the huge blossoms at a flower stand, the dyed yarn of a wool vendor, and the peaches, lemons, and oranges on a fruit cart.

Jane wandered off a few yards to browse through Indian print scarves that fluttered from a rope. Bess stopped Nancy by squeezing her arm.

"Jane's been through so much," Bess said. "And now with the Hardys accusing her of stealing Angelique's material, I'm afraid she's going to snap under the pressure."

"The guys have good reason to suspect Jane,"

Nancy explained. "She's definitely tied in to Skyler, Inc., and you know about all the trouble they've been having."

"How can they accuse her of faking amnesia? *I* was the one who bonked her on the head!" Bess exclaimed.

"Bess—" Nancy tried to calm her friend.

"And what about the guy who tried to smother her?"

"Bess," Nancy said, "none of us wants to see Jane implicated in the embezzlement. But we have to get to the bottom of this. I find it hard to believe Jane is involved, but we have to accept the possibility."

"I guess you're right," Bess said wearily, as they moved on through the airy marketplace.

The three were about to leave when a woman called to them. At first Nancy wasn't sure what to make of the woman sitting at a table covered by a fringed umbrella. With her dark ponytail, cut-off jeans, and baggy T-shirt, she could have blended in with the crowd if it weren't for her cat's-eye sunglasses trimmed in sparkling rhinestones.

Taped onto the table was a sign that said: Tarot Card Readings By Madame Santini—$5.

"Hey, girls," she called. "How about a reading? You can look into the future, or learn a few things from the past."

Nancy was about to decline when Bess snapped her fingers and said, "Great idea!" She motioned Jane over to the table. "Can you really see the past in those cards?" she asked the woman.

"Sure." Madame Santini eyed Bess and Jane. "Who wants to go first?"

"Go on, Jane," Bess insisted, reaching into her purse for money. "My treat. Maybe Madame Santini can help you remember things."

"I don't know." Jane hesitated. "The idea makes me nervous."

"Sit down and relax, honey," the woman said. She stuffed the money into the pocket of her shorts, then pushed the cards across the table. "As you shuffle, think of a question you want to ask. The answer will be revealed in the cards."

Reluctantly, Jane took a seat and picked up the cards. "Should I tell you my question?"

Madame Santini's dangling copper earrings jingled as she shrugged her shoulders. "If you want, but you don't have to."

Closing her eyes for a moment, Jane shuffled the cards. "I guess I'd like to know what happened last Monday."

Bess and Nancy stood behind Jane's chair, watching curiously.

"Okay," the woman said. "We'll focus on Monday, but a few of the cards will reflect the future. Now cut the cards."

Jane separated the cards. Then Madame Santini quickly swept them away, counted out ten cards, and began to turn them over and position them into a cross shape on the table.

Having seen tarot cards before, Nancy knew they were different from playing cards. Each card had an illustration and a title. The pictures of castles and the costumes worn by the people depicted told Nancy that the cards' designs had been created hundreds of years earlier.

Although Madame Santini was silent as she turned over the cards, Jane read the title of each card aloud. "The Moon. The Ace of Wands—"

"Aren't aces good?" Bess asked.

"Maybe," said Madame Santini shortly, annoyed by the interruption.

"The Three of Pentacles," she continued. "The Five of Wands. The Tower. The High Priestess—"

"She looks like a queen," Jane said.

Nancy was fascinated by the cards. One showed an ancient stone tower that was being struck by lightning and beginning to crumble. Among the falling rocks was a king, tumbling to the barren ground.

Another card showed a man hanging upside down, his feet tied to a tree. Despite his position, he didn't look unhappy.

Nancy realized she was eager to hear what the cards meant, or at least what Madame Santini thought they meant, even though she was a little skeptical.

"One more card," Bess said. "I can't stand the suspense."

But the image on the final card sent a chill shuddering through Nancy. It showed a skeleton in a suit of armor. He rode atop a white horse that was trampling a fallen king.

Jane gasped, then lifted a hand to cover her mouth.

"Oh, my gosh," Bess said breathlessly. "It must be the Death card!"

Chapter

Eighteen

Y ES, IT IS the Death card. It's in your future,"
Madame Santini said as her eyes traced the entire
spread of cards.

Swallowing hard, Jane asked, "Does that mean
I'm going to—"

"Die?" The fortune-teller glanced up at the
solemn faces of the three girls, then shook her
head. "No, not at all. It's a good card—especially
good, considering its placement in the spread.
The Death card also means transformation. See
this king on the ground? He's fallen, making way
for a new regime. The destruction of his kingdom
will be followed by renewal."

Jane sighed, obviously relieved by the woman's explanation. "What does that mean in my
life?" she asked.

"Your life is going to be transformed. You're
trying to make a new start." Madame Santini

swept her hands over the other cards. "But I can see from these cards that it hasn't been easy. Monday was a rotten day for you."

"I'll say," Bess interjected.

"See this card?" Madame Santini pointed to the Tower card.

Jane studied the card, then nodded.

"The Tower means catastrophic change. Something started to crumble in your life on Monday, something involving greed and deception," the woman explained, pointing to the Moon card.

Then she tapped the Five of Wands, a card showing five men in the heat of battle. "There was a battle on Monday—a violent fight. You ran from it, which was the right thing to do. There are other people in this reading, and they are the guilty ones—not you."

"I knew it," Bess said, nudging Nancy.

Madame Santini pointed to the Knight of Pentacles, and Nancy saw that it was a dark-haired man holding a gold coin. "There's a dark-haired man connected with money. A laborious, patient man. He is involved in the wrong-doing."

Was it Mario Slick? Nancy wondered, totally involved with the reading by now. Or maybe it was the accountant, Gary McGuire? Wasn't accounting laborious, painstaking work?

The fortune-teller tapped a card that showed a man sculpting a design. "This is the card of the master craftsman. I can see that you are very talented and involved in the arts."

"That's true," Bess said. "She's a singer."

Then Madame Santini pointed to the card showing the hanging man. "But right now you are suspended, like this man. This is a waiting period for you. You will be helped by this person." The card she indicated showed a woman who resembled a princess. "Do you know who this is?"

Jane studied the card showing a beautiful woman with coiled red hair. "I'm afraid my memory is a little fuzzy."

"It's someone you know now," Madame Santini said. "Someone with hidden influences. She is the link between the seen and the unseen world."

A smile lit Jane's face as she turned to Nancy. "It's you, Nan. You're a detective, working behind the scenes to help me."

"Could be," Nancy agreed, intrigued.

"Just one word of warning," the reader warned. "Beware of a man—an older man—driven by greed. He created the deception that caused this trouble. This is him." She pointed to the Devil card, which showed a fiery demon.

"He looks gruesome," Bess said.

"Now." Madame Santini gathered up the cards and shuffled them once. "Who's next?"

"Where are they?" Frank asked as he paced the posh lobby of the Astor Towers.

"Calm down," his brother said, lifting his sunglasses to watch two pretty girls walk up to the front desk. "It's only four, and we weren't supposed to meet them until six."

"I hate to think of Nancy and Bess wandering around with a girl who—" Frank stopped abruptly when he saw Bess come through the revolving doors. "Here they are."

"This is a surprise," Nancy said. "For once, you're early. Come on up."

"You'll have to excuse Jane and me while we rehearse," Bess insisted.

"No problem," Frank said. He was eager to talk to Nancy—alone.

Up in the suite Jane and Bess settled down at the piano, while the Hardys settled in at the table in the dining room.

"If you guys wasted an afternoon waiting in our hotel lobby, you must have something hot to share," Nancy said as she closed the door and sat at the head of the table. "What's up?"

Frank told her what they had learned from Special Agent Thornberg, stressing the trust account set up in Jane's name. "For some reason, Crockett lied to us. I'd love to know why he wanted us off the case."

"Maybe you were upsetting Angelique," Nancy suggested.

"No way," Joe insisted. "You saw the way she acted with me. She likes me."

Frank rolled his eyes and said, "Maybe she wants you to *think* she likes you."

"Or maybe you hit a nerve," Nancy said thoughtfully. "You found something—or you were getting close to something that Crockett wanted to remain hidden."

"If only we knew what that was." Frank rubbed his brow, concentrating. "I'd also like to know if Jane Orbach is on the level. There are two million dollars stashed away in the Cayman Islands in her name."

"So you think I'm the thief," said an angry voice from behind Frank.

"Jane—" Nancy was surprised to see the subject of their conversation standing in the doorway. She hadn't noticed that the music had stopped. "Nobody is accusing you of anything. Right, Frank?"

"That's true," Frank said, turning around to face Jane. "All we want to do is get to the bottom of this mess. I'm sorry if it sounded otherwise."

Jane looked as if she'd been stung. She swallowed hard, then said, "It's okay." She tossed a small black datebook on the table. "Anyway, I came to show you this."

"Jane," Nancy began gently, "Special Agent Thornberg said that you might not be connected to the stolen money. Someone else could have set up the account in your name."

"So I heard. But I'm sick of being in the dark about my life." Jane spun toward Frank, her eyes shining with tears. "I've got to find out the truth—even if it means that I'm a criminal."

Bess appeared in the doorway a moment later. "I heard, too," she said sheepishly, then turned to Jane. "I really want to prove that you're innocent."

"We all do." Frank held up his hands with the palms out. "How can we help you?"

"I need to confront the people at Skyler, Inc.," Jane said. "But I'm afraid of what they might do to me." She turned to Nancy. "I have to find out who the devil was in that card reading."

"What are you talking about?" Joe asked.

Nancy filled in the Hardys on some of the statements the tarot card reader had made.

"A fortune-teller?" Frank said, frowning. "I don't think that'll hold up in a court of law."

"The point is," Jane said, "Madame Santini jolted my memory. Now I can piece together some of the dates in that book."

"Where did you find this?" Nancy asked as she leafed through the slim datebook.

"It was in the pocket of my jacket," Jane explained. "But nothing in it made sense until now. The appointments were all written in abbreviated form."

Nancy turned to Monday's date. Blank. She flipped back to three weeks earlier and found some letters and numbers penciled in. "Okay," she said. "Three weeks ago you wrote Sidewalks —ESS—9PM. Any idea what that was?"

Jane smiled. "ESS is Electric Sound Studios. I had an appointment there at nine P.M."

"Wow," Bess said. "Do you remember what happened at the studio?"

Jane's voice rose in alarm. "I went into the studio to record the vocal track for— 'Sidewalks.'"

Joe shook his head, confused. "That's the song from Angelique's album."

Jane nodded. "That's why I know all of her material." Then, in a voice barely above a whisper, she said, "You're looking at the voice and brains of the legendary Angelique."

Chapter

Nineteen

W AIT A MINUTE." Joe stared at the dark-haired girl in disbelief. "We know Angelique, and you don't look anything like her."

"But she *sounds* like her," Nancy said as the puzzle pieces began to fall into place. "Doesn't she?"

Bess's blue eyes were bright with hope. *"And* she knows Angelique's songs. Did you write all the material for her albums?"

"I think so," Jane said. "But I'd have to see a list of the songs to be sure."

"I saw a few of Angelique's CDs in the living room, next to the stereo," Joe said. "Hold on a second and I'll get them."

Frank studied Jane thoughtfully. "If you actually wrote and recorded Angelique's material, then what does she do?"

"She's beautiful and has a great body," Jane

said slowly. Then she burst out, "But she's never been able to sing—at least not in public. Whenever they film a video, she lip-syncs. And she's never done a concert tour, for fear the audience will figure out that she's a fake."

Joe returned with two of Angelique's compact disks, announcing, "All the songs are written by Angelique and copyrighted under Skyler, Inc."

"Which means," Bess said, "if Jane wrote the songs, she wasn't given credit—or royalties."

Jane studied the titles listed on the covers. "They're my songs. I *know* it."

Nancy's mind raced ahead. If Jane's memory was accurate, then Jane and Angelique had been perpetrating a hoax. Who else would know about it? Crockett and Veronica would have to be involved. There must be others, too—or maybe not, since Angelique recorded the vocals in secret.

She was convinced that Jane's role in the scam had something to do with the fact that someone was trying to kill her. Before she could consider that link, she needed to know if Jane really was the voice of Angelique. There had to be some way to prove it.

"I'm glad your memory's coming back," Nancy told Jane. "But we've got to find a way to prove this." Leafing through Jane's datebook, Nancy found ESS—Electric Sound Studios—penciled in a few times. "If only we could find someone who saw you at those recording sessions."

"That's impossible," Joe pointed out. "Fish told us that Angelique's vocals were always recorded in secret, closed sessions."

"Fish! That's it," Nancy exclaimed, spreading the datebook flat on the table so everyone could see. "Even if he was closed out of the sessions, he could find out when they were scheduled. Because studio time is so expensive, recording studios have to be very careful about scheduling."

"That's right," Frank said, his face lighting up. "We can call in these dates to Fish, and he can check and tell us if they match up with the studio time booked for Angelique's vocals."

Frank called Electric Sound Studios and was lucky to find Fish in. "I need you to give me the dates and times of Angelique's last sessions," he said to his friend. Fish read off the answers from a studio calendar.

"We've struck gold," Frank told the others, smiling.

The group was ecstatic—except for Joe, who sat sulking in his chair. Frank guessed that his brother had been hit hard by the news about Angelique, now a fallen star.

When Frank explained the situation to Fish, the engineer didn't seem surprised. "That explains why even I wasn't allowed into Angelique's sessions."

"Who *was* around when Angelique's vocal tracks were recorded?" Frank asked.

"Crockett and Duke."

Before he hung up, Frank invited his friend to join the group for dinner, but Fish had to turn him down.

"I'll be working through the night," Fish told him. "We're putting together the rough mix for a jazz album. But if you're in the mood for some entertainment, check out the Howling Coyote. It's talent night, and a lot of the producers will be there, scouting new acts. You'll probably run into Crockett. Maybe Veronica, too."

When Frank hung up, Bess was handing out sodas. He popped open a can and took a sip, then noticed that Nancy was lost in thought.

"There's still a lot we don't know," she said. "We need to find out who's trying to kill Jane— without giving them another chance to hurt her."

"And we need to find out who embezzled that money," Frank added. "There are two million big ones in an account with Jane's name on it. If you didn't put it there, Jane, somebody else did."

"I don't remember anything about any money or the Cayman Islands," Jane insisted.

"We might be looking for the same person," Nancy said, snapping her fingers.

"That's true," Joe said. "The would-be killer could easily be motivated by that amount of money."

"I have to get to the bottom of this in order to clear my name." Jane gripped her soda with determination.

Nancy knew they had better find answers fast, because the closer they came to solving the case, the more danger Jane would be in. She kept her thoughts to herself. "I want to go back to your apartment tomorrow to hear what the tenants have to say about your landlord. Maybe we'll find a clue we overlooked."

"In the meantime," Frank said, "we may be able to shake the truth out of Crockett Skyler or Veronica."

"What do you mean?" Bess asked.

"Fish tells me that Crockett and Duke engineered the vocal tracks on Angelique's albums," Frank explained.

"Which means those guys have to be in on the scam," Joe said excitedly.

"And I know where they're spending the evening." Frank smiled mischievously. "Time to hatch a plan. Brace yourself, Jane. Tonight, you just might be giving the performance of your life."

"I'm so nervous," Jane said, sipping a glass of lemonade while the others finished off their desserts of bananas flambé topped with whipped cream. "I'm not sure I'm comfortable performing in front of an audience this large."

There was standing room only at the Howling Coyote, a Mexican restaurant in Greenwich Village. Luckily, the teens had been able to get a large round table since they'd come for dinner before the crowd gathered.

"You'll be terrific," Bess assured Jane. "You're one of the best singers I've ever heard. And I really appreciate all the help you've given me with my act for 'Rising Star.'"

Bess and Jane had spent the remainder of the afternoon refining Bess's song-and-dance routine for the next day's studio rehearsal. By the time they finished, even Joe and Frank knew Bess's song about the football player by heart, and everyone was starving.

Glancing around the restaurant with brightly striped Mexican serapes draped along the walls, Frank caught sight of Veronica and Mario sitting at a small table. Were they counting the days until they flew to the Cayman Islands to retrieve the stolen money? he wondered. He had promised Thornberg he wouldn't press them, and Frank Hardy was always true to his word.

Joe seemed to be staring off into space. Following his brother's gaze, Frank saw he was really looking at Angelique, who was sitting at a table behind the rail on the upper level. Behind her, Crockett and Duke stood talking with five or six others in a cluster.

"Time to bait the trap," Frank muttered.

Joe frowned. "You know, Angelique's only seventeen. You can't blame her for getting caught up in this scam."

"No one's blaming anyone," Nancy pointed out. "We're just here to see how certain people react to hearing Jane sing songs from Angelique's albums."

Three acts later, Jane was called to the stage.

"We'll be right here if you need us," Nancy said as she and Bess walked Jane up to the edge of the stage.

Frank and Joe headed over to the stairs leading to the upper level. Frank wanted to get a closer look at Crockett's reaction, and Joe was hoping for a chance to talk with Angelique.

"I'd like to sing a song from Angelique's first album called 'Blue Lightning.'"

The minute Jane spoke into the microphone, Joe saw that Angelique went pale. He dashed up the four steps to the upper level and sat in the empty chair across from her.

"Hey, gorgeous," he said, smiling.

Angelique didn't seem to notice him. Her face was a frozen mask of shock as she stared at the girl on the stage. It was clear to Joe that Angelique was reacting to more than the song.

"Recognize the singer?" he asked.

When Angelique turned to him, tears sparkled in her brown eyes. "I'm sorry," she said, her voice cracking with emotion. "I can't talk to you now." She snatched her purse and stood up, cutting through the crowd and disappearing out the exit.

Meanwhile, Frank was struggling to get closer to Crockett and Duke, the two men he was certain had secretly recorded Jane's voice at Electric Sound Studios. The tightly packed crowd refused to move as everyone stood stock-still, staring, transfixed, at Jane.

Crockett muttered something to Duke, and the younger man scowled.

At last a guy moved and Frank edged through the opening he had left until he was directly behind the two men. He'd been planning to eavesdrop, but a shove from behind jostled him against Duke's shoulder, and the younger man spun around to face him.

"Watch it, man," he snapped, then squinted. "Oh, it's you."

Crockett seemed surprised to see Frank. "Still in town, Hardy?"

"My brother and I decided to stick around to take in the sights." He nodded toward the stage. "What do you think of tonight's talent?"

"The young lady's got quite a voice," Crockett said pleasantly. "Of course, she doesn't do my daughter's material justice. And I wish she'd stop going around town imitating Angelique."

"Maybe you should speak to her," Duke said. "Set her straight." From the way his jaw was clenched, Frank could see that Duke was angry.

"No, son." Crockett slapped Duke on the back. "You catch more flies with sugar than with vinegar. The way to stop Miss Jane Orbach from imitating my daughter is to give her a better offer. Maybe ask her to do some background vocals."

Frank was surprised. He hadn't expected the record producer to take this so well. Could it be that Jane was lying? But what about her datebook?

Crockett turned and slipped a beefy hand onto Frank's shoulder. "Duke here's a little worked up. Why don't you do me a favor and give that singer my card. If she's interested in working for me, she can come out to my summer place on Long Island and get to know my staff. We're having a little party on Friday to celebrate Angelique's eighteenth birthday."

"I'll give her the message," Frank said.

"You and your brother and friends are welcome to come, too," Crockett added. "The more the merrier."

When Jane finished her song, Nancy and Bess cheered along with the crowd. Jane was beaming as she left the stage and joined the girls.

"You're *better* than Angelique," said a guy standing next to them. Jane smiled modestly and lowered her eyes.

Frank met them at the side of the stage and suggested they leave to find a quiet place to talk. Outside, the night was warm. Music and laughter wafted through the Village streets on the summer night air.

A slight breeze lifted Nancy's reddish gold hair as she and Frank led the group. "Why don't we get a cold drink here?" she suggested, stopping beside an outdoor café lit by strings of little white lights. Round tables with vases of flowers were set up along the sidewalk.

"This place looks perfect," Frank said. He and Joe pushed two of the small tables together. Five minutes later a waitress returned with a tray of frozen fruit drinks decorated with paper umbrellas and plastic mermaids.

"A star is born." Bess clinked the glass of her peach frappé against Jane's lemon slush.

"Dynamite performance," Joe agreed.

"Thanks," Jane said, her face still glowing. "I liked performing, though I kept thinking that someone was going to run onstage and steal my mike."

"Well, you really upset Angelique," Joe said, explaining how the girl had stormed out.

"On the other hand," Frank said, "Crockett was cool as a cucumber. He even invited us to a party at his house on—"

He was interrupted by an explosion. The flower vase on their table had burst into pieces, the water and flowers littering the tabletop.

"What was that?" Bess cried, shielding her face with her hands.

"A gunshot!" Joe shouted. "Get down, everyone!"

Chapter

Twenty

SOMEONE'S SHOOTING AT US!" a man shouted as tables and chairs went flying and people crawled behind café furniture or scattered into doorways.

Shrieks pierced the air, and tires screeched on the street as cars took off to get out of the line of fire.

Huddled behind a downed table, Frank heard a second bullet whiz by. Nancy crept over beside him. "Did you get a look at the gunman?" she asked.

"No," Frank admitted, pushing over another table to use for cover. "All I saw was a gun jutting out of a doorway. It's a revolver."

"That means he probably has four shots left before he needs to reload," Joe whispered.

A third bullet sent splinters flying off a nearby chair.

"He's going to kill us!" Jane cried, her voice shrill. Jane's haunting image of a gun was a reality once again, Nancy thought, pitying the young woman.

Jane frantically started to crawl away, but Joe pulled her back behind a table. "Wait him out," he ordered.

Four! Frank counted as another shot rang out.

Five! The bullet made a pinging sound as it hit the metal base of one of the tables. "That was close," Frank said. "Either his chamber is empty or he has one more bullet."

"Let's see." Joe grabbed a chair and, remaining hidden behind an overturned table, lifted the chair over his head.

A moment later a sixth gunshot rang out. The bullet banged into the chair, the force almost knocking the chair from Joe's hands.

"Let's get a look at the gunman before he has a chance to reload," Joe said, tossing the chair aside.

Joe and Frank dashed out from the sprawl of tables and chairs. "Stay here," Nancy ordered Bess and Jane, then raced off behind the guys.

"There he goes!" Frank cried as he and Joe rounded a corner. He pointed to a tall man dressed all in black from his baseball cap to his sneakers. The man caused a screech of brakes and blaring horns as he ran into the direct path of a yellow taxi.

Seconds later Frank and Joe were darting between the same cars.

"Easy does it," Joe said, patting the hood of the cab and racing onto the crowded sidewalk.

As soon as Frank cleared the traffic, he saw that the man had led them into a maze of people and outdoor vendors.

Under the pockets of light from street lamps, Frank saw that St. Mark's Place was teeming with activity. Racks of merchandise covered the sidewalk space not filled in with shoppers and tourists.

Out of the corner of his eye he saw someone dressed in black duck behind a rack of sunglasses. He crept up behind the guy and was about to grab him when he turned around. It wasn't a guy, though—it was a woman, definitely not the shooter. Frank sighed in frustration and continued looking. "Where'd he go?" he muttered.

Joe, meantime, was searching through racks of T-shirts dangling on hangers. He saw plenty of bins of shoes and books and twirling racks of greeting cards, but no sign of the shooter.

When Nancy joined them, they systematically combed the street again, but there was no trace of the gunman.

"I never got a look at the guy's face," Joe said, frowning. "You couldn't see a thing under that baseball cap."

"He was dressed like the guy who tried to smother Jane," Nancy pointed out.

"All we know is he's tall, with broad shoulders," Frank said.

"Which doesn't narrow it down much," Nancy said. "From that description, it could be Crockett, Mario, or someone unknown to us. This is frustrating."

When they returned to the café, the staff was sweeping glass and righting tables. A crowd had gathered around a uniformed officer who was listening to Bess describe the scene as a waiter took off running after two patrons. "Hey, come back here and pay your bill!"

Teary-eyed, Jane was sitting on the steps of the shop next door.

"Are you okay?" Nancy asked.

Jane nodded. "The police have been interviewing witnesses. Fortunately, no one was injured. But it scares me to think of what could have happened. I can't believe anyone would shoot on a crowded street—" She brushed tears from her cheeks.

"We'll get this guy," Nancy vowed. "Somehow."

Early the next morning Nancy, Bess, and Jane met the Hardys for breakfast at a restaurant overlooking the leafy green trees of Central Park.

"Today's my official rehearsal at 'Rising Star,'" Bess said, her blue eyes wide. "The first hour or so is just warm-up, but then we'll start to rehearse with the cameras. Promise me you'll be there by eleven."

"I promise." Nancy smiled as she buttered a slice of toast. "I need to fill in Detective Lebowitz on the latest incidents. Then Jane and I are heading over to her apartment building. We'll go to the studio as soon as we're finished there."

"What about you guys?" Bess asked.

"I want to check in with Agent Thornberg," Frank said, "but that shouldn't take too long. We'll be there before you go on stage."

Half an hour later Nancy and Jane were canvassing Jane's apartment building on the Upper West Side. They had just started knocking on doors on the third floor when they met a thin, middle-aged man in a business suit. "Hi, Jane," he said. "I was just on my way to work."

"Hello," Jane said, smiling. "I'm afraid I don't remember your name. I've been suffering from a memory lapse since Monday."

"Did you see the shooting on Monday?" Nancy asked him.

He told her that he'd been at work Monday morning, and he agreed that Tony Caruso was a difficult man.

"The guy's a little crazy. Of course in our cases he's worse"—he nodded at Jane—"since our apartments are rent controlled. The landlord could charge a lot more rent for them if he could get in new tenants, so he'd love to get rid of us."

"So that's why he wants me to leave," Jane said, explaining what the landlord had said to them.

"He can't do that," the man insisted. "You have a lease. Tony's bluffing."

After the man left for work, the girls worked their way down to the first floor, where they found an elderly woman at home.

"I've seen you around, dear," the white-haired woman said as she squeezed Jane's hand. "And I was here on Monday when that awful man tried to shoot you."

"Did you see him shoot the gun?" Nancy asked.

"No, but I heard the gunshots echoing through the stairwell." The woman clutched her chest, adding, "Thought my heart would give out. Then I saw him running down the stairs—through here." She pointed to a peephole in the door.

Nancy put her eye up to the round glass and saw that it was focused on the stairs. From this angle, the woman could have seen the gunman fleeing. "What did the man look like?"

"I couldn't see his face," the woman admitted. "But he was wearing the most interesting cowboy boots. Turquoise boots."

Turquoise cowboy boots! That had to be Crockett, Nancy thought. He always wore a cowboy hat and Western gear.

"Thanks," Nancy told the woman. "You've been a big help." Now we just need some solid evidence, she thought.

By the time Nancy and Jane arrived at Rockefeller Center, it was crowded with tourists and business people. Nancy used a pay phone in the lobby to check in with Lebowitz. Then she and

Jane rode the elevator up to "Rising Star"'s studio.

Frank and Joe were already sitting in the audience.

"You guys are setting a bad precedent—being early all the time," Nancy teased as she and Jane sat down.

A rap trio called Kross-I's was onstage. They were one of the four acts, including Bess's, that would appear on TV. Nancy had to admit their rap song was great, and their dance steps even better. She saw that three cameras, each the size of a refrigerator, were being wheeled around the stage to shoot the scene from different angles.

"Any luck downtown?" Nancy asked quietly after the act was over.

"Not much," Frank said. "Thornberg booked an agent on the same flight as Veronica and Mario. He'll monitor their activities in the Cayman Islands. Other than that, nothing to report."

Nancy told the guys what they'd learned from Jane's neighbors. "The cowboy boots made me think of Crockett—though, of course, it's not solid proof. I did learn that Tony Caruso is not our gunman. I just talked to Lebowitz, and the ballistics evidence says the slugs in Jane's door came from a .38 revolver—the same type of gun as Tony's, but not the same weapon."

"How could the police lab tell without Caruso's gun?" Joe asked.

"He surrendered it," Nancy said, suppressing

a giggle. "When Caruso was approached by Detective Lebowitz, he turned soft as a marshmallow." She turned back to the stage and said, "Oh, look! She's on."

Bess was standing in the middle of the stage, beaming and waving at her friends in the bleachers while the lighting crew made their adjustments.

The director instructed Bess to start off standing on a gray X taped to the stage floor. "That's your mark," he told her. "As long as you start off your routine from there, the cameras will be able to follow you."

"Gotcha," Bess said, jumping on top of the X.

The director cued her, and Bess started singing.

Nancy watched as one camera operator wheeled her huge camera across the stage to get a profile of Bess. Meanwhile, the camera with the red tally light was moved in for a close-up of Bess's face. Bess did her routine twice, running through it each time without a hitch. The director thanked her. "Great job," he said. "We'll see you here Saturday morning for the taping."

Outside, Nancy saw a patch of deep blue sky bordered by tall buildings. The square plaza was rimmed by colorful flags, which flapped in the summer breeze. She followed the others to the railed area overlooking the center of the plaza. Used as an ice-skating rink in the winter, the lower level was now an outdoor café.

"What a gorgeous day," Bess said, still charged up from her rehearsal.

"We have the afternoon free," Frank said, eyeing the café filled with tables shielded by umbrellas. "Why don't we have lunch here while we figure out a game plan?"

A waiter showed them to a table next to a fountain. They ordered salads and sandwiches, then Nancy sat back and basked in the sunshine.

"I've got to run to the ladies' room," Jane said, placing her napkin on the table.

"It's inside." Nancy pointed to the smoked-glass windows of the restaurant.

"Be back in a second," Jane said, smiling. Nancy and Bess watched as she wove a path through tables and disappeared inside.

"Jane is doing much better," Nancy said.

Bess nodded as she sipped an iced tea. "I'm glad her memory is returning. If she—"

Just then they all heard a bloodcurdling scream come from inside the restaurant.

Nancy's heart leapt to her throat as she jumped up from the table. "That's Jane!"

Chapter

Twenty-One

FRANK RAN and plunged through the doorway. He couldn't see for a moment until his eyes adjusted to the dim room.

He was in the restaurant's bar area, which was deserted but for an alarmed-looking waiter behind the bar. Two people were wrestling against the wall on his right.

"Leave me alone!" Jane shrieked, struggling to free herself from the man's grasp.

"Hold on!" he insisted, refusing to release her. "You don't understand—"

The man shifted, and Frank got a good look at his face. He'd seen the dark-haired man with the round glasses before. It was Skyler, Inc.'s accountant, Gary McGuire.

"Gary!" Frank exclaimed. "What are you doing?"

Taken by surprise, he released his grip. Jane slipped away and stumbled over to Nancy, who had followed Frank in. Gary regained his balance and adjusted his glasses.

"I was on my way to the ladies' room when he jumped out of the shadows and grabbed me," Jane accused.

"But I didn't—" Gary began, obviously flustered. "I was just trying to—I mean—"

"Hold on a second," Nancy said. "Calm down, both of you, so we can straighten this out."

The Hardys returned to their table with Gary, and Nancy and Bess accompanied Jane to the ladies' room before rejoining the guys.

"I'm sorry if I scared you," Gary told Jane. "Ever since the guys brought that photo of you around, I've been wanting to talk to you before I told them what I know." Leaning forward, he lowered his voice and added, "You see, I know the truth about you—that you're the real Angelique."

Confusion crossed Jane's face. "I don't remember you at all," she admitted.

"I saw you at Electric Sound about six months ago," Gary explained. "One night I brought Crockett some papers to sign. I went into the studio, and you were in there alone, rehearsing a song.

"You didn't notice I was there, but once I heard your incredible voice, it didn't take me long to figure out the whole thing. When I couldn't find your name on the accounts, I realized that Crockett must be paying you a ridiculously low fee out of his petty cash fund."

That explained why Jane had so much cash in her apartment, Nancy thought.

"And all the time the Skylers were making millions from *your* talent," Gary said angrily. "This business makes me sick."

"But why did I let Crockett and Angelique take advantage of me like that?" Jane asked.

"After you finished the song, I came up to you and asked you," Gary started to explain. "You told me you were shy, scared to death of audiences. You were trying to overcome the fear, with acting classes."

"And I first agreed to do it because I needed the money and the work. I remember that now," Jane said.

"Did anyone else see you in the studio?" Joe asked Gary.

"No. And Jane begged me to keep her secret. She said there'd be trouble if anyone found out that Angelique was a fake. I ducked out and waited for Crockett in the reception area."

"But why did you sneak up on me just now?" Jane demanded, still unsettled.

"I happened to be eating here. When I saw you, I had to talk to you. I've been wanting to ever since I saw your picture." He turned to the others, explaining, "I wasn't sure how much you knew, and I'd heard that Crockett had taken the Hardys off the case. Personally, I don't trust anyone right now. That includes the people at Skyler, Inc. If Crockett realized that I knew his daughter was a fraud, he'd chew me up and spit me out."

Nancy studied the accountant as he spoke. He'd spooked Jane, but he wasn't Jane's attacker —at least, he wasn't the man who had sneaked into her bedroom or come after her with a gun the night before. The attacker was taller, with much broader shoulders.

"Are we still friends?" Gary asked with a hopeful smile.

Jane's face was blank. *"Were* we friends?"

"Well"—Gary hesitated, then answered—"sort of. After we met I made a point of being at Electric Sound when I knew you were recording. Sometimes, when you were on breaks, we'd talk."

"I'm sorry," Jane said, shaking her head. "But I don't remember you. And after what I've been through this week, I panicked when you jumped out and grabbed my arm."

"I would never hurt you," Gary insisted. "The truth is, I like you, Jane. I never had the nerve to tell you before. Maybe I came on a little strong inside, but when I heard you'd lost your memory, I thought you could use a friend."

"I appreciate your concern," Jane said politely. "But right now I just have to rely on the bits and pieces that I do remember."

"I understand," Gary said. "If you need help, though, you can count on me."

"Thanks," Jane said as Gary got up to leave.

"Are you going to confront Crockett now?" Nancy asked Jane.

Jane's expression told everyone at the table that she wasn't willing to do that yet. "I will— soon," she said slowly. "But please don't force me to do it now. I'm still too afraid, and I feel that I need to get my *whole* memory back first."

"But—" Bess started to protest.

"Please," Jane pleaded. "Let me handle it my way, okay?"

Nancy and Frank nodded, and Nancy said, "Okay, Jane—whenever you're ready, we'll be there to back you up."

"Thanks," said Jane, smiling.

Just then the waiter returned with a tray of salads and sandwiches. As they ate, Nancy mulled over what Gary had said. Suddenly a new thought occurred to her.

"Remember what the tarot card reader said yesterday about that card with the man holding a gold coin?" Nancy asked Bess and Jane.

Bess swallowed a bite of salad and nodded. "She said there was a dark-haired man connected with money. Someone with patience."

"Who does that remind you of?" Nancy prodded.

"Gary McGuire," Joe said, putting down his sandwich. "What else did the reader say about him?"

"That's one thing I *do* remember," Jane said.

"She told me he was involved in the wrongdoing."

Nancy saw the skepticism on Frank's face. "Interesting," he said. "Though I wouldn't rely on a fortune-teller's advice."

"Frank Hardy," Nancy said, "plenty of police departments have used the help of psychics to solve crimes. So what's wrong with heeding Madame Santini's warning?" she teased.

"Nothing," Frank said, grinning. "But I'd rather stick to good old-fashioned logic."

Bess suggested that they take the subway downtown and spend the afternoon on the Staten Island Ferry. "The boat goes past Ellis Island and the Statue of Liberty," Bess explained, "and it's only fifty cents round-trip."

Everyone agreed that it was the best way to enjoy the clear, sunny day. They paid their lunch tab, then walked to the subway station. Frank bought tokens for everyone, while Nancy asked a transit officer for directions to the downtown train.

"Turn right and go down the stairs," the cop said, "but there might be some delay. The last I heard, that line was running late."

As Nancy led the group down the stairs to the train platform, she saw that there was a huge cluster of other people waiting. Most of them kept glancing at their watches and then down the train tunnel.

As they walked to the far end of the platform,

where it was a little less congested, Joe said, "At least we're not in a rush."

As they waited, they discussed the invitation to the birthday bash at Crockett's summer house.

"I've seen pictures of that house in magazines, and it's incredible," Bess said. "There's an in-ground, indoor pool and a gazebo for outdoor concerts."

Just then Nancy was jostled forward by someone bumping into her. Glancing behind her, she saw nothing but impatient and bored faces.

Frank stepped up to the yellow line at the platform's edge to peer down the tunnel. He said, "He made a sham of his daughter's career. What else is he hiding? This embezzlement case is going to bug me until I have all the answers."

"I feel the same way," Jane said, "and I have more at stake."

Looking down the tunnel, Nancy felt a blast of hot wind on her face. "The train is coming at last."

"How far do we ride this train?" Bess asked as the lights appeared at the far end of the tunnel.

Nancy reached into her tote bag for her subway map and felt more movement behind her. Several people were speaking at once, their voices rising over the train's rumble.

Nancy glanced up just in time to see a gloved hand reach out and shove Jane forward.

"Help!" Jane cried as she flailed her arms and legs in midair, then plummeted onto the tracks —right in the path of the oncoming train!

Chapter

Twenty-Two

Nancy saw Jane lying in a crumpled heap on the tracks. Could she make it back onto the platform before the train arrived?

"Jane!" Nancy shouted, rushing to the very edge of the platform. "Give me your hand, quickly now."

Jane rolled into a sitting position, then stood up, wavering queasily on her feet.

"Hurry!" Bess shouted, kneeling beside Nancy.

Frank spun around and searched through the crowd for the person who'd pushed Jane. "He was tall," one witness volunteered, "and he went that way." The guy pointed down the platform. "That's him! That guy in black."

Frank saw a tall man in dark clothing with a black baseball cap dart toward the stairs, pushing his way through the crowd.

"Stop him!" Joe shouted, shoving through people in pursuit of the man. Frank raced off beside him.

Meanwhile the train was moving closer. "Please, Jane, hurry," Bess pleaded.

Frantic, Nancy reached a hand out for Jane, who was finally too overwhelmed to act.

The shrill screech of the train's brakes jolted Nancy into action. Trying not to think about the train that was almost upon them, Nancy jumped down onto the tracks and grabbed the hysterical girl.

"Step over the third rail," she shouted, pointing to the raised rail that ran parallel to the tracks. Nancy knew the third rail, which supplied power to the trains, carried enough electricity to kill a person.

Nancy pulled Jane to the far side of the tracks as the train lights grew larger and caught them in a hot white glare that drained them of all their color.

Sucking in their stomachs, they made it out of the train's path moments before the train rolled into the station.

Then, when the train pulled out and after making sure no other train was on the way, the girls moved back to their platform, where at one end they found a built-in metal ladder. They scrambled up, then hugged each other in relief.

"You saved my life," Jane said breathlessly.

Within seconds Bess was at their side. "I was

so worried about you two," she said, throwing her arms around both girls.

Joe and Frank chased the culprit all the way to the subway exit, but lost him on the crowded street.

"Suddenly I have no interest in riding the subway," Bess said after they were questioned by the transit police.

"Let's go back to the hotel. We can get cleaned up and plan a new agenda," Nancy said.

"Maybe we should catch a Broadway show," Frank suggested.

"Fine with me," Bess said. "I've had enough real-life drama to last me awhile."

The following morning Frank woke with the nagging feeling that he'd missed something.

Propping his pillow up behind him, he sat up in bed and thought about the case that he and Joe were no longer working on. There had to be a way to trace the funds from Skyler, Inc.'s New York account to the trust fund in the Cayman Islands.

Frank rubbed his eyes, then noticed the hefty computer printout sitting on the dresser. Gary had sent it there by messenger, but Frank hadn't looked at it since that day in Gary's office.

Glancing at the clock, Frank saw that it was just after eight. Joe was still asleep, and the party at Crockett's didn't start till one. What was the harm in going over Skyler, Inc.'s account one more time?

Three hours later Frank was reading the last few pages of figures as he and Joe arrived in front of the Astor Towers in a rented car. Nancy was waiting outside, dressed in a blue sundress that brought out the color of her eyes. Bess and Jane emerged from the lobby to join them.

"We're going to the north shore of Long Island, not Hawaii," Bess teased Joe as the girls piled into the back of the car. Seated behind the wheel of the convertible, Joe was decked out in sunglasses, swim trunks, and a pink shirt dotted with palm trees.

"Crockett said to dress casually," Joe said. "By the way, does anyone know how to get to this place?"

"I checked the map this morning," Frank said, pulling it out of the console. "Take the Midtown Tunnel and I'll direct you from there."

They drove through the tunnel, then merged onto an expressway.

"I hope you girls are ready for some fun," Joe called out to them in the backseat. "Frank's been a dud with his nose buried in printouts all morning."

Nancy grabbed the back of Frank's seat and leaned forward. "Find anything?"

"Maybe." Frank circled a number, then held up the printout so Nancy could see it. "There's a definite pattern in these withdrawals, which are actually transfers to the PIKA trust account in the Cayman Islands. Each withdrawal came just a day after funds deposited were cleared."

"What does that mean?" Bess asked.

"Whoever took this money knew the exact status of the Skyler, Inc., account," Frank explained. "They knew when the funds were clear and exactly how much they could siphon off without overdrawing the account."

Nancy's blue eyes flashed with excitement. "So it's got to be someone on the inside, like Crockett or Veronica."

"Who didn't seem to be keeping a close watch on their finances," Frank pointed out. "After what happened yesterday, I'm more inclined to think that the thief is Gary McGuire."

"Could be," Joe said. "He knows the status of Skyler, Inc.'s account."

"And Crockett trusted Gary," Frank said, nudging Joe. "Remember the day we were in Gary's office and he gave Crockett papers to sign?"

"That's right." Joe snapped his fingers. "Crockett signed off without reading them."

"Considering the fact that Gary has a crush on Jane, it makes sense," Nancy said thoughtfully. "When Gary learned that Jane was the real talent behind Angelique, he couldn't stand to see Crockett take advantage of her. Gary then began to siphon off the money so he could give it back to Jane. He opened a trust account in her name."

"And, from these statements, the embezzling began about the same time that Gary learned you were the voice of Angelique," Frank said.

Jane bit her lip, worried. "Do you think I was his partner in the theft?"

"I sure hope not," Frank said, "but I'll find out. I'm going to confront Gary at the party, try to bluff him into confessing. Unfortunately, we don't have any hard evidence."

"But Madame Santini described him," Bess said.

"That would hardly hold up in a court of law," Frank said wryly.

"She also told us to watch out for a devil," Nancy said thoughtfully. "I wonder if that's Crockett."

"I don't know about the Devil card," Frank said dubiously. "But even if Gary is the thief, we know he's not the man who's chasing Jane."

"Right," Nancy agreed. "So we need to catch the would-be killer. My money is on Crockett Skyler. Maybe you wanted out of the scam, Jane, and Crockett was afraid you'd expose him to the press."

Joe was thoughtful for a moment. "Didn't Lebowitz confirm that the bullet holes in Jane's door came from a thirty-eight?" When Nancy nodded, he smacked his forehead. "How could I have forgotten! I saw a thirty-eight in Crockett's briefcase the day I met him."

"On Monday?" Frank thought back to the meeting. "That was the day Jane's door was shot up—and Crockett was late for the session," Frank said excitedly. "When he finally got there, he was winded and sweating. And that morning no one knew where he was."

"So he *could* have gone right from Jane's apartment to the studio," Nancy said.

"But Crockett's not the guy stalking Jane," Frank said. "The attacker is a tall guy with broad shoulders—leaner than Crockett."

"Right," Nancy said. "Maybe Crockett has a sidekick. That description fits Mario—"

"Though I don't think *they'd* work together on anything," Joe said. "But you never know."

Jane shivered, despite the warm day. "Suddenly I'm not looking forward to this party."

As Joe turned up a tree-lined driveway, music and voices filtered out through the woods. Rounding a curve, they reached a clearing that gave them a clear view of Crockett's spectacular estate.

Nancy saw groups of people milling around on the perfectly groomed green lawn. In the center of the lawn was an octagonal gazebo, a wedding cake of a structure trimmed with flowers. At the far end of the lawn, the water of an aqua pool sparkled as guests volleyed a beach ball.

"Surf's up!" Joe said, grinning.

The main house resembled a Victorian mansion. Painted gray, the three-story house was trimmed in lavender woodwork with spiked peaks over every window and door. There was a porch that turned into a bridge at the far end. The bridge looped over a narrow lap lane of the pool that disappeared into the sunroom of the house.

"It's like a gingerbread castle!" Bess exclaimed as Joe parked between two sports cars.

"Does this place look familiar to you?" Nancy asked Jane as they climbed out of the car.

Jane shook her head. "I don't think I've ever been here before."

"Welcome!" someone called from the lawn.

Nancy saw Duke Powers, looking right at home in a white tennis outfit.

"Crockett asked me to show you around," Duke said. "He's inside talking with Slade Landon."

"The rock star?" Joe asked.

Duke nodded. "Slade is going to sign with Skyler, Inc. He's doing a few songs today to get the party going. I've already miked the gazebo."

"Slade Landon," Bess said dreamily, a smile lighting up her face. "I can't wait to meet him."

"Where's the guest of honor?" Nancy asked.

Glancing around to make sure no other guests were listening, Duke answered, "Angelique is up in her room, sleeping. Crockett says she's having a bad reaction to that medication for her larynx. It was too late to postpone the party, though. Personally, I think she's just mad about being upstaged by Slade."

Everywhere Nancy turned there were tables of refreshments. There were racks of grilled shish kebab that made her mouth water, dainty sandwiches, and fountains of fruit punch.

As they strolled along the grounds, Duke pointed out the pool house, where guests could shower and change. They took the curved bridge over the pool to enter the solarium.

On the far side of the solarium, the pool lane emptied into a circular wading pool built into a deck overlooking Long Island Sound. The deck, which ran along the waterfront side of the house, jutted over the cliff a hundred feet above the rocky beach. At the west end of the house, Nancy noticed a wooden staircase that led down the cliff to a boat house.

"If you look across the sound, you can see Connecticut on the horizon," Duke said, leaning on the balcony rail. Then he checked his watch and frowned. "It's time for Slade's show. I'd better double-check the sound system in the gazebo."

"Just lead the way," Bess said.

Out on the lawn, Frank saw Crockett onstage in the gazebo. He was talking to a short man with long brown hair whom Frank recognized as Slade Landon. Everywhere he looked, Frank recognized celebrities. Where was Gary McGuire? he wondered.

At last he spotted the bespectacled man near a buffet table, a platter of shrimp in one hand.

"There he is," Frank said, nudging his brother. "I think it's time to go over some figures with the accountant."

When the Hardys approached Gary, he agreed

to talk with them. He led them to a quiet room in the west wing of the house.

Glancing up at the antlers mounted on the wall, Joe said, "Looks like Crockett is a hunter."

"It's all for show," Gary said, pointing at the walls. "Crockett has never set foot in the woods —or on a ranch. The man's a fraud in every way."

"But Crockett was honest about one thing," Frank said, facing Gary squarely. "He didn't siphon money out of Skyler, Inc. You did."

"Don't be ridiculous," Gary snapped. "If I were dishonest, I'd have been booted out of my profession years ago."

"Maybe you didn't think it was wrong when you first started transferring the money out," Frank said. "You thought it was the noble thing to do, since the money wasn't for you. It went into an account for Jane Orbach, the girl who wrote and performed Angelique's songs but got just a few thousand dollars for her talent and genius."

Gary coughed on a shrimp, then sputtered, "Tell me another."

Frank saw that Gary was beginning to crack. Now was the time to really press him. "You want more? Okay. Funds were deposited into the Cayman account just one day after they'd cleared Skyler, Inc.'s account. Aside from the bank itself, *you* are the only one who had access to that information. Plus you provided printouts that show that the embezzlement started when you learned that Jane was Angelique's voice."

Now beads of sweat were breaking out on the accountant's face. "I—I—" He started to respond, but Frank cut him off. "And Joe and I witnessed the way Crockett signs anything you put in front of him. You did it. Admit it now, there's no way you'll get away with it."

"Okay," Gary whispered, burying his face in his hands. "I did it." After a long pause, he looked up and said, "Jane deserved those millions—not Crockett, not Angelique. I fell in love with her the night I heard her singing. She didn't know about the money. She didn't even know I was in love with her," he finished sadly.

Frank picked up the phone from Crockett's desk and punched in Paul Thornberg's number.

While Frank filled the federal agent in, McGuire sighed and said to Joe, "You might as well know, it was me who cut the sound and lights at Angelique's concert."

"What for?" Joe asked.

The accountant mopped his brow and said, "I knew Angelique was lip-synching that night. I thought that if I sabotaged her performance, everyone would see she was lip-synching. I know, it was a stupid idea, and obviously it didn't work as I planned."

"But how'd you know what to do?" Joe asked.

"I watched Duke set up the generator that ran all the electrical juice to the concert. All I did was cut the main line when Angelique was in the middle of a song. No one was around—they were all focused on her singing," Gary explained.

Just then Frank hung up and said, "The police cruisers will be here soon. I guess you know you'll have to stand trial for—"

A muffled cry from out on the deck made Frank halt in midsentence. In the next instant the loud rock music of Slade Landon began pouring through the speakers.

"Did you hear that cry?" Frank asked Joe. His brother's nod was all he needed. Frank ran to the window that overlooked the deck.

At the end of the deck, just a few feet from the wading pool, Frank saw two people struggling.

It was Crockett. He had Jane around the waist and was pressing a gun to her temple. Frank realized he must have timed his attack on Jane down to the second that Slade's music started, when everyone would be on the lawn out front and no one could hear her scream.

As Frank watched, Crockett dragged Jane to the balcony railing and threw her against it.

Only a thin wooden rail stood between Jane and the rocky beach a hundred feet below.

Chapter
Twenty-Three

I T'S CROCKETT—he's got Jane," Frank shouted, and raced toward the door. "Keep an eye on McGuire," he barked over his shoulder.

As Frank ran down the hall to the deck door, his mind raced to come up with a plan. With the crowd watching Slade perform in the gazebo, the house was empty. If Frank didn't stop him, Crockett would succeed in killing Jane!

Just as he turned the corner of the hallway to get to the door, he saw a young woman standing in its threshold.

It was Nancy! She was speaking slowly to Crockett, who still had an arm around Jane.

Staying out of Crockett's sight, Frank waved and caught Nancy's eye. "I'll go around—behind him," he mouthed, gesturing. Nancy's barely perceptible nod told him she understood.

Quickly Frank ran to the east wing of the house, pulled off his shirt and shoes, and lowered himself into the narrow lap lane that would lead him to the wading pool behind Crockett.

Meantime, Nancy took a deep breath, willing herself to remain calm. "Take it easy," she said softly. "There's no reason to hurt Jane."

Crockett shoved Jane hard onto the deck. She landed in a sobbing heap at his feet. "Quiet," he growled. "Both of you." He waved his pistol at Nancy. "You have been the bane of my existence all week, never letting Jane out of your sight."

Until today, Nancy thought, frowning. She had been sitting beside Jane, waiting for Slade Landon's show to start, when Jane said something about going inside the house for something. Why didn't I go with her? Nancy chastised herself. Somehow Crockett had gotten to her.

Now Jane began creeping away from him, toward Nancy, but Crockett only laughed. "Go on. Run to the detective. She can't protect you now." He wiped the beads of sweat from his brow and sighed. "It was going to be nice and simple. A distraught singer jumps to her death. No one would question it much. After all, the girl has amnesia."

Never taking her eyes off Crockett, Nancy bent down and helped Jane to her feet.

"Now I'm going to need another method," Crockett said. "Two jumpers are suspicious."

"You don't need to kill us," Nancy said, trying

a new tack. "Jane can go on being the talent behind Angelique. Let her finish the third album, and you'll be a rich man again."

"Angelique's career is over," Crockett snarled. "My daughter can't handle fame anymore. Why do you think she's hiding upstairs? No, Angelique's career is going to end with permanent larynx problems. And Jane's career is going to end—along with her life. I've just signed a deal to produce Slade Landon's next album, and there's no way I'm going to let Jane Orbach spill the truth and ruin my career."

"Just tell me one thing," Jane said, taking a deep breath. "Why wouldn't you let me out of the deal? Why did you try to kill me?"

From the sharp look in Jane's eyes, Nancy sensed the girl's memory rushing back.

"You were demanding to be recorded in your own name. If you didn't get recognition, you said you'd go to the press. I couldn't have that, could I?" Crockett's eyes flashed dangerously. "And it was *me* who nurtured your voice into a money-maker for all of us!"

As Crockett ranted, Nancy saw a head slowly emerge from the wading pool behind the producer. Frank! She had to keep the gunman distracted.

"Crockett," she said, bluffing, "the police know everything." She stared straight at the man, trying not to think about the dripping wet figure that was creeping up behind him.

"They know all about the scam you pulled with Jane," Nancy said. "They have witnesses who—"

"Ugh!" Crockett groaned as Frank wrenched the man's gun hand skyward, then landed a karate kick to his lower back. Crockett crumpled forward.

With a clatter, his gun skidded away. Nancy leapt forward and snatched the gun up while Frank pinned the groggy producer down.

"You girls okay?" he asked over his shoulder.

Nancy nodded and slipped an arm around Jane's shoulders. "Another close call, but we're all right." She smiled down at Frank, his wet hair dripping onto Crockett's back. "Nice trick, Hardy."

Nancy heard a clicking noise behind her that made her stomach twist. It was the sound of a gun being cocked.

"An excellent trick," said a familiar male voice. "Too bad it will be your last."

Slowly, Nancy, Frank, and Jane turned to see Duke Powers behind them with a cocked revolver. Nancy's fingers tightened around the gun in her hand, but Duke swung his gun toward her and scowled.

"Move and I'll shoot," he said. "Move away from Crockett," he ordered Frank, who obeyed. He didn't dare try anything with a gun pointed at Nancy and Jane.

Crockett scrambled to his feet and snatched his gun back from Nancy.

"I missed you before," Duke added, "but I was shooting in the dark."

"You were the one who shot at us at that café," Nancy said. How could she have missed it? With his broad shoulders and lean build, Duke matched the description of Jane's stalker.

"Yours truly." Duke smiled. "I only meant to scare you that night. I wanted you to back off so Crockett and I could get closer to Jane."

"I suppose you were the subway phantom, too," Frank said, eyeing the young man.

"People get so pushy in subways," Duke said. "And then there was the time I paid you that bedtime visit," he added, leering at Jane. "I should have killed you then. I would have, if it weren't for your meddling friends."

"The balcony gig won't work anymore," Crockett told Duke.

Nancy realized that Slade's concert would be ending soon. People would be wandering around the grounds. How long could these guys keep waving guns around?

"Let's take them down to the boat house," Duke said. "There's enough gasoline down there to blow up half of Long Island."

"But people will hear the explosion," Crockett pointed out.

"That will make good headlines. 'Teens die tragically in explosion. Too bad they were playing with fire.'" Duke began to laugh as he and Crockett directed Nancy and the others to the end of the balcony.

Nancy felt queasy as she stared down the treacherous steps—four sets of wooden stairs zigzagging precariously down the cliffside. It was hopeless. To jump off the staircase would be suicide, and the beach was so rocky, they couldn't hope to get far.

At gunpoint, the men escorted Nancy, Frank, and Jane down the stairs and into the clammy darkness of the boat house. Three speedboats bobbed there in the calm black water.

"Sit here," Crockett ordered, pressing Nancy down on a bench beside Jane. He tied the girls' wrists together behind their backs.

As Duke tied Nancy's feet together, she searched Frank's face. What can we do? But there was no answer in his dark eyes.

Gasoline fumes stung Nancy's eyes as the men flung the liquid fuel around the building.

"This place is a tinderbox," Frank muttered, looking up at the wooden rafters and walls. "It'll go up in seconds."

"That's the idea," Crockett said with a wicked grin, as he finished tying Frank's wrists. "Happy trails, kids. Thanks for making the party such a blast." Pouring a trail of gasoline to the door, the men left the boat house.

"We don't have much time," Jane said, her voice betraying her hysteria. "One match and we're history."

Frank stood up and hopped along the dock. "What about swimming out?" he asked.

"Jane and I are tied together—we'd drown,"

Nancy said, trying to keep the desperation out of her voice. That was when a shiny piece of metal in one of the boats caught her eye.

"A key!" she gasped. Someone had left a key in the ignition of the speedboat. "Quick, we've got to get in!" she cried. "Jane, on the count of three, we'll hop toward the boat."

"I'm scared," Jane whimpered.

"It's our only chance. We do it," Nancy said, "or die trying."

Back inside the house, when five minutes had passed with no sign from Frank, Joe knew something had gone wrong. He'd walked to the window in time to see Duke and Crockett forcing the others down to the beach. Joe quickly used the curtain ropes to tie the accountant to Crockett's desk chair and tore down the hallway to the door.

Outside, he leaned over the rail just in time to see two figures race out of the boat house and clamber behind a boulder.

It was Crockett and Duke. He guessed that the men had locked Nancy, Frank, and Jane in the boat house.

Then a giant fireball exploded on the beach.

One second Joe was staring at the boat house.

The next, he was staring at a trembling wooden frame enveloped in yellow flames.

"Frank! Nancy! Jane!" Joe shouted.

Chapter

Twenty-Four

N o!" Joe shouted.

The boat house burned, and a cloud of thick black smoke rose up from it. Somewhere in those flames and smoke were the bodies of his brother, Nancy, and Jane.

As Joe watched in horror, a movement beyond the black haze caught his eye. It was a boat, and it was racing wildly away from the shore.

Inside the boat were three people. Could it be Nancy, Frank, and Jane?

Joe grinned as he recognized Nancy's bright blue sundress. It was them! They had gotten out of the boat house before the explosion!

Then he turned his attention toward Crockett and Duke, who were halfway up the staircase to the deck. They didn't seem to have noticed the runaway boat.

As he peered outside, he was surprised to see

Angelique scuffling across the deck. Although she was wearing a robe, she was shivering, and her hair was tousled.

"What's going on, Daddy?" she asked, rubbing her eyes. "I heard a loud bang, and—"

"It's nothing," Crockett barked. "Go back to bed. You don't want the guests seeing you like this, do you?"

"I'm not a baby." Angelique pointed to the gun sticking out of Duke's waistband. "Did you shoot someone?" When the men didn't answer, she persisted. "Tell me what's going on!"

Joe stepped onto the deck beside Angelique. The two men sneered as he faced them. "Your father just murdered Jane Orbach, the singer who recorded your albums," Joe said flatly, not willing to tell them that their plan hadn't been successful.

"Murder!" The color drained from Angelique's face. "Daddy, tell me it's not true."

Crockett just shrugged. "It was for your own good, honey," he said, raising his gun to Joe. "And if you'll just step inside, I'll take care of the last of the troublemakers."

Eyeing the barrel of Crockett's revolver, Joe could feel his heart race as the man took aim.

"No!" Angelique threw her arms around Joe to shield him from her father. "Daddy, have you lost your mind? You can't go around killing people to get what you want."

"Stand back, Angelique," Crockett barked. "Let me finish what I've started."

"I wouldn't do that if I were you!" a man called from behind Joe.

The shout was followed by a series of double clicks that Joe recognized as the sound of rifles being cocked.

Crockett's smile faded. A moment later, he and Duke lowered their guns.

"Drop 'em."

Joe turned around and saw that the order came from a sheriff standing in the doorway with a couple of other officers.

Joe could hear the shouts of party guests. The explosion had probably sent them running toward the house.

Remembering the boat lingering offshore, Joe raced to the edge of the deck and motioned his brother in. At last they'd cracked their case.

"All right!" Frank cheered.

Joe let out a shrill whistle, and Nancy and Jane clapped as Bess took her second bow. Her performance for "Rising Star" had been flawless.

Now it's up to the judges, Nancy thought as Bess blew kisses to the audience and ducked behind the stage curtain.

During the commercial break, people in the audience whispered excitedly.

"You know," Frank said, "it's hard to believe that Bess missed all the action yesterday. She's usually right in the heart of things."

"She was totally engrossed in Slade Landon's performance," Nancy said.

"Along with all the other guests," Joe pointed out. "No one would have known anything strange was going down if Crockett and Duke hadn't blown up the boat house."

"I know this will sound strange," Jane said, "but yesterday's events jarred my memory completely. I remember why Crockett was chasing me on Monday." She frowned. "He'd promised me a legitimate recording contract but never came through. I'd finally worked up the nerve to appear in public and was ready to start my own career. Crockett kept putting me off, though. Finally, on Sunday, I called him and said if he didn't give me the contract on Monday, I'd go to the press. Monday was when he tried to kill me. I guess he figured the only way to silence me was to kill me—even if it meant the end of Angelique's career."

"How did the scam start?" Joe asked. "Can't Angelique sing at all?"

"She can, but she's not great, and wasn't willing to work at lessons. Crockett decided to cash in on Angelique's main asset—her charisma."

"She does have that," Joe said grimly, remembering how attracted he'd been to her.

"Crockett and Duke are being charged with attempted murder. They'll probably spend a long time in jail," said Frank.

"I wonder why Duke got sucked into the whole mess," Nancy said.

"He was motivated by greed," Joe explained.

"Duke told Thornberg that Crockett had given him a percentage of the profits from Angelique's albums to make sure he kept the situation under wraps. Duke was willing to do anything to move up in the record business. He even tried to knock me off at the video shoot. Thornberg found out that Duke removed the bolts, then gave the lamp a shove when I walked by."

"He deserves to do big time," Frank said, shaking his head. "Though it looks like Angelique and Veronica won't be charged. From what the police told me, they're accessories in the scam but didn't know anything about the attacks."

"I wonder what will become of Angelique," Joe said wistfully. "She did save my life, you know."

"We'll read all about her in the next issue of *Rolling Stone*," Frank said. "They're doing an article called 'Angelique's Masquerade.' In fact, a reporter called our hotel room asking for an interview."

"They called me, too," Jane said. "They want Angelique and me to appear on the cover."

"From what Angelique said before we left her father's house yesterday, she'll be much better off now," Nancy said. "She told me that the strain of living a lie was too much to bear."

"What's going to happen to Gary?" Jane asked.

"He's cooperating with the feds, a hundred percent," Joe said.

Frank nodded. "The embezzled funds will be returned to Skyler, Inc., although the company will be under investigation, too. It will take a while to figure out who gets what, but I think Jane will get part of that money."

"Crockett's career is over," Nancy said, turning to Jane, "and yours is just beginning."

Joe was confused. "Did I miss something?"

Jane smiled. "Yesterday, when you were helping with the police report, I was approached by Slade Landon. He heard the whole story and asked me to think about teaming up with him."

"That's great," Joe said.

"I'm definitely going to write some songs for him," Jane said. "But I'm not sure I want to take on a partner. I have to think about it."

"And I'm sure other offers will come your way after that *Rolling Stone* article comes out," Frank said.

Just then Brandon Winkler returned to the stage and the applause sign flashed.

"We're proud to announce the winner of this week's competition," Winkler said brightly.

Nancy held her breath and waited for the TV host to go on. Bess had been great, but so had the other three acts. The rap group called Kross-I's had brought down the house, and so had a jazz pianist.

"The winner is—Kross-I's!" Brandon Winkler shouted.

The audience cheered as the rap group returned to the stage and took a bow.

When the taping ended, Nancy and the others went backstage to see Bess.

"Thanks for all your help, coach!" Bess said, hugging Jane. "I would never have made it onto the air without you."

Nancy was glad to see that Bess wasn't too disappointed by the results of the "Rising Star" competition.

"My pleasure," Jane said.

"Maybe you could give me a few pointers sometime," Joe said, eyeing the guys who had won the competition. A dozen girls had sneaked backstage and were vying for autographs. "I think I could do a mean rap tune."

Frank rolled his eyes. "You're kidding, I hope."

Joe nodded his head rhythmically, chanting, "Now Joe's the name, mystery's the game—"

Everyone burst into laughter.

"What's so funny?" Joe insisted as his face turned red.

Bess clapped Joe on the shoulders. "New York audiences are tough to please," she said, smiling. "Ever think of taking your act on the road?"

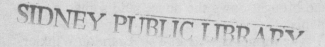